Wasabi for Breakfast

Two Novellas

OTHER WORKS BY FOUMIKO KOMETANI
IN ENGLISH TRANSLATION

Passover

WASABI FOR BREAKFAST
TWO NOVELLAS

FOUMIKO KOMETANI

Translated by Mary Goebel Noguchi

DALKEY ARCHIVE PRESS
CHAMPAIGN / LONDON / DUBLIN

Originally published in Japanese as *Family Business* by
Shinchosha, Tokyo, 1998

Copyright © 1998 by Foumiko Kometani
Translation copyright © 2013 by Mary Goebel Noguchi
First edition, 2013

Library of Congress Cataloging-in-Publication Data is available.
ISBN: 978-1-56478-864-1

This book has been selected by the Japanese Publishing Project
(JLPP), an initiative of the Agency for
Cultural Affairs of Japan

Partially funded by a grant from the Illinois Arts Council,
a state agency

www.dalkeyarchive.com

Cover design by Mikhail Iliatov; illustration by Foumiko Kometani

Printed on permanent/durable acid-free paper

FAMILY BUSINESS

1

Oharu-baasan complicates. That's what my relatives say whenever I go back to Japan, "*honma ni yayakoshii*"—she runs around in circles, complicating things. But since I live in America, I haven't had to deal with all the trouble she causes. Until now.

I'm a fifty-eight-year-old Japanese woman, a wife, a mother, an artist, living in Los Angeles. My career as a painter, however, is in Japan, where I have been lucky enough to have gallery shows in Tokyo and Osaka every other year. I fly back to Japan frequently, and my first priority upon arriving is to set up appointments with gallery owners to show them transparencies of my recent work.

Upon landing at Narita at the start of my latest trip, I take the train into Tokyo and then a taxi to my son John's Roppongi apartment, letting myself in with the key he's given me. Every time I come back to this tiny, overpriced hole-in-the-wall, I find myself getting all tensed up. The first time I came to stay here, I opened the front door and saw another door right in front of me, just two meters away, and, thinking that there was a room on the other side, I opened it. I was quite disappointed to find that it was just a closet, the back side of which was the outside wall of the building.

My son, who's a freelance photojournalist, has been living here for some time now, but I've timed my trip to Japan to coincide with his return to the States so that I can have the apartment to myself.

The next day, just after the luggage I sent from the airport has been delivered by parcel service and I am in the midst of unpacking, the telephone rings.

A clear voice speaking in a thick Kansai accent comes over the line. "*Moshi moshi*. When did you get in? You said you'd be getting in late yesterday, so I didn't call then. Are you free tomorrow?"

It's my eighty-seven-year-old mother, Oharu-baasan. For Oharu-baasan, my homecoming means nothing more than my appearance in the course of her daily life, but for a middle-aged woman who has just arrived in the country—that is, for me —it's a different matter. I was in the midst of taking out shoes, stockings and blouses still steeped in American air and dusting out my suitcases. Despite my having packed them myself two days ago I found their presence here, outside their usual environment in my closet in Los Angeles, disorienting. I am in that uncomfortable yet familiar state of just having returned, stuck between nations, Japan and the United States, between languages, between cultures. Yet Oharu-baasan won't understand why I can't tell her if I am free tomorrow, nor is there any way I can explain it to her.

I can't explain it to myself.

"Ahh, *genki*?" I greet her in Kansai-ben, asking how she's doing. "C . . . c . . . could you hold on a minute?" I stutter, yet the dialect, at least, is reassuringly familiar.

I was born and bred in the Kansai area of Western Japan, where I grew up speaking the regional dialect. Whenever I come to Tokyo from the United States, I am initially tongue-tied as I

try to switch from the round, broad vowels and dropped consonants of a foreign language—English—to a rapid-fire, carefully
enunciated alien dialect—the Tokyo style of Japanese. But the
Kansai-ben begins flowing from my lips the moment I hear it. At
the same time, I am wondering to myself how I can stave off my
mother, thinking, "*Komatta naa*—this is bad; this is bad . . ."

Without waiting for me to answer, Oharu-baasan continues,
"Other than tomorrow, I'm . . . let me see: the middle of next
week would be good. It's just that a group from here is talking
about going on a trip, and I'm going with them. It'll be for five
or six days, so you see, I've got a schedule to work around, too.
Let me know as soon as you can when a good time would be.
You know, you let me stay in that apartment the last time you
were here, but I also stayed there another time after that when
John asked me to come and stay with him."

"Oh?"

"How's Ken?"

"Oh, he's doing pretty good these days, though you never
know what's going to happen."

Ken is our second son and he was born with severe autism.
The only reason I've once again become productive as a painter
was his placement in a state hospital a few years ago.

"Well, I feel better now that I've heard your voice," she says,
lowering her tone to a somewhat calmer pitch.

"Then, tomorrow at . . ." I start to say, but Oharu-baasan has
already hung up.

I guess people feel pressed for time when they get older.

The nickname Oharu-baasan is a combination of my mother's
first name, Oharu, and the Japanese word for grandmother,
obaasan. Her grandchildren began calling her this as a joke, but
somehow the contraction stuck. Oharu-baasan used to live in

the Tezukayama area of Osaka, but when my father died, she sold their house and began seeking a retirement home in Tokyo near my brother, who is four years older than me. For some time now she's been living in an elderly care facility on the outskirts of Tokyo that allows her to come and go as she pleases. She's in good health and chose this place herself after visiting almost a dozen times, so as I see it, she's not really in a position to complain about it.

I've been away in the United States for half a year and I know that Oharu-baasan is eager to see me. She would also like to see my American husband, David.

She has asked me in the past why I don't bring him. I told her I avoid coming to Japan with him whenever possible.

I'm sure those of you who are married to someone who speaks a different native language will understand why I do this. Thirty years ago I became one of the first Japanese to enter into what is known by that odd term, "international marriage." David is well over sixty, and while there may be lots of Americans of his generation who pride themselves on their mastery of, say, French, there are not many outside missionary or diplomatic circles who could be commended for their efforts to learn Japanese like Donald Keene did (and even Mr. Keene's Japanese competence was largely the result of American military requirements during the war). Anyway, David can't speak much of any foreign language. "International" couples of our generation who live in America manage their affairs by having the foreign spouse learn English. I imagine the younger generation is different. There are plenty of young Americans who speak Japanese well, so there's no need to go out of your way to translate for them. Also, it's not like we're newlyweds, for whom the initial excitement of being married to a foreigner and introducing him to my native city, culture and language has yet to wear off. We were like that once—all young and green and doing our best to promote intercultural exchange. What I'm referring to here is more like a couple that's green with mold.

Instead, when we visit Japan now, I become a translator, and am also forced into other mind-numbing roles—from cultural attaché to pop psychologist to behavioral scientist. I'll be all set to enjoy dinner with friends, only to find myself making excuses for America to my Japanese friends while, at the same time, interpreting my Japanese friends for David, who sits dumbly at my side. While I'm translating, everyone else is enjoying the meal, leaving me to gulp down the glorious repast so quickly that it leaves a bad aftertaste.

I prefer to eat slowly.

The last time David came back to Japan with me, my younger sister, Chizu, Oharu-baasan, David and I were standing in the middle of a street in the trendy Shinsaibashi shopping district in Osaka when we started talking about what we should eat for lunch. Thinking that we should consider David's opinion, too, I asked him what he wanted. He told me to ask Oharu-baasan first. In the meantime, the old lady and Chizu got sidetracked talking about some book or other, and Grandma said that she would borrow the book from Chizu. Then suddenly, as if he'd hit on a good idea, David began walking around looking at the wax models of food lined up in the restaurant display windows, and when he found a curry restaurant, he told us all to go in. The rest of us were talking about something else, so we just went along with him into the restaurant. Chizu and I were content to have curry, but when the food was brought to our table, Oharu-baasan, who never has an opinion about anything, suddenly blurted out, "I don't want that!"

David got angry and demanded, "Then why did you say 'curry roux' a few minutes ago?"

Oharu-baasan's face went blank. "Did I say I wanted to eat curry? I don't remember that."

Nobody had any idea who had first suggested curry.

Chizu burst out laughing.

"I was thinking about what Grandma and I were talking about before we came into the restaurant. She said she was going to borrow a book—*hon wo kariru*. David must have heard *kariru* as 'curry roux' and figured we were talking about curry, so he went ahead and decided that that's what we were going to eat!"

And there I was, caught in the middle, translating my husband's previous mistranslations back into Japanese, and then vice versa. What can I say? I have no way of knowing what Japanese David is picking up, and he often doesn't understand what he's listening to anyway. After thirty years of marriage, my tolerance for interacting in two languages at once has worn thin, and taking vitamin B_6 or E or whatever—all the potions that are supposed to stimulate brain activity—has about as much effect as a magic incantation.

In ancient Japan, Prince Shotoku was praised for his intelligence because he was able to listen to ten people simultaneously and understand what each was saying, but I imagine they must have all been speaking Japanese. Moreover, I believe he was young when he died—probably not over fifty, anyway. If the ten people had been speaking two or three different languages, I can assure you that even Prince Shotoku would have ended up ignoring nine of those ten speakers.

That's why I like to come to Japan when my son John goes back to America. When he's there, he and his father do nothing but talk in English for twelve hours straight every day. If I come to Japan while he's home, I not only escape having to listen to them, but I also get by without having to translate for David.

2

We eventually arranged for Oharu-baasan to stay with me overnight at the apartment. Not that she could come here on her own. It seems that when she visited John, he had met her at my brother Yoshio's home in Suginami, since she knew how to get there by herself. I was reluctant to make a similar plan, knowing Yoshio would have to go through all the trouble of feeding her and putting her up the night before. Instead, I arranged to meet her at the second most familiar place for the two of us: Shinagawa Station.

When I finally spotted her at the station, Oharu-baasan seemed a different species than the taller, youthful, hurried commuters all around her. She was short, and hunched over, she appeared even smaller as she tottered along with her protruding belly and black skirt. Her yellow hat was tipped back on her head, and beneath its brim she wore sunglasses that looked like dragonfly eyes. A black-and-white carryall sack she had woven herself was slung over her shoulder and she carried a cane under her arm. I almost missed her, but she looked so strange—not because of her age but because of a generation-defying weirdness—that I couldn't help but notice her.

"Why are you holding a cane like that? Isn't that dangerous?"

I felt momentarily guilty that even though I hadn't seen my mother for quite a while, my first words to her took the form of a reprimand rather than a considerate greeting; however, I'm getting older too, and these days I find that if I put off saying something, I forget to say it at all.

"Everybody says, 'Take a cane, take a cane,' so I take one," she proclaimed in her thick Kansai accent. "But anyway, I don't understand why we had to meet in a place like this. I can't stand such *yayakoshii* places! We could have met on the platform of Naka-Meguro Station, you know, there on the Hibiya line— there're a lot fewer people there, and it would have been much more convenient. But I guess it couldn't be helped—you don't know anything about Tokyo."

What could I say? She made it sound like she had to put up with a lot of extra trouble just because I was "half foreign" and didn't know anything.

The apartment was too close to take a taxi, so when we got to Roppongi Station, I had to make her walk. It was just the opposite of what we'd done when I went shopping with her as a child; then, it was her pulling my arm, with the sleeve of her kimono flapping in my face, making it hard for me to breathe. In those days, she had been thin and rather on the tall side.

I walk slowly these days; my mother walks even slower. We stayed out of the way of fast-walking, youthful pedestrians and delivery boy bicycles streaking by on the sidewalk and finally made our way to the apartment building. Since the apartment is on the second floor, I grabbed her under the arm and practically had to pull her up the stairs.

Heaving a sigh, Oharu-baasan dropped herself down in a chair in the living room, taking her hand-woven bag off her shoulder and putting it on her lap. As soon as she sat down, she began talking, but since I'd gone to the kitchen to put water in the teakettle,

I couldn't hear her. I turned on the burner under the kettle.

Although I call the little area walled off from the living room a kitchen, it's only about two mats wide—less than three square meters—with a refrigerator, gas stove and sink. I've put on some weight recently, so when I was using the stove, it felt quite cramped. I wondered how my son, who's twice as big as I am, could possibly move around in there.

When I reemerged from the cubby-hole kitchen, my aging mother pulled a piece of dark blue wool cloth with green stripes on it out of her bag and, waving it up and down in her right hand, said, "Here, give this to David. I wove it to pass the time."

"My, my! This is a—oh, you really shouldn't have," I said.

She'd handed me a piece of roughly woven wool cloth about the size of an old album jacket.

"This is a . . ." I studied it. "What is it?"

"A muffler, of course."

Thinking that it might be mean to blurt out the obvious design flaw, I demonstrated my doubts by putting the "muffler" on my shoulders. It was so short the ends didn't cross at the neck.

"It was kind of you to weave it for David, but it's way too short for a muffler. David is so big. It might work if it was at least ten centimeters longer."

"Too short? Then don't tie it."

"A muffler doesn't stay on if you can't wrap the ends around each other."

"Then use it as a tablecloth."

A wool tablecloth? There was nothing I could say to that, so I just went back into the kitchen to make the tea. Clearly, she hadn't lost her ability to think very quickly at times like this. During World War II, Japan's scarce resources had forced housewives like my mother to find uses for everything, and it seems that even now, she hasn't gotten out of that mindset. With the world's population growing so quickly, we're bound to face another period of shortages again, so if my mother lives long enough, she'll become a really valuable member of society once more.

I brought out the tea and some Daifuku rice cakes with red beans in them that I'd bought earlier.

"You know, I can't eat stuff that sticks. I've got false teeth in front, and they don't really fit."

I'd been hearing this same complaint for the last three years. "Weren't you going to go to a new dentist? Last year when I was here you were saying that."

"Every time I go to my regular dentist's office, there's a different dentist."

"Yes, but didn't Yoshio's wife say she found a good private dental clinic? Didn't you go there?"

"I would have had to take the train. So I just told the neighborhood dentist to make these fit better. It didn't do any good."

Now I could understand why my older brother and his wife and my younger sister and her husband, who live in Shuku-gawa near Kobe, got so fed up listening to my mother complain about how she needed them to find a dentist for her.

"There's nothing we can do about that now, so why don't you just take out your dentures and put them on that *tissue* and then eat the rice cakes."

"What's a *tissue*?" she asked, confused by the English word I'd used.

"That Kleenex," I used another English word familiar to most Japanese under the age of eighty-seven.

"What are you talking about?"

"That—*chirigami!*" I said, finding the old-fashioned Japanese term for tissue paper. I had become quite flustered because I couldn't come up with the Japanese word.

"Oh, but if I take my dentures out, I won't be able to chew the rice cake, and it'll get caught in my throat. Is there anything else?"

"Oh—yes, some French cookies John left."

"They must have butter, cholesterol. I suppose it doesn't matter at my age. I could die at any time now. Oh yeah—speaking of death—I just remembered: The Buddhist ceremony for the third anniversary of Auntie Ikuyo's death is going to be held in Kamakura next week. Why don't you come with me?"

"When is it?"

"This Sunday. It's not for another four days."

I thought it might be nice for me to go in order to make my mother look good. David wasn't along, so there would be no need to serve as translator. And I had missed Auntie Ikuyo's funeral. She was Oharu-baasan's younger sister, so my appearance at her memorial would make my mother look better to my cousins. If I didn't go, someone would probably later mention to my cousins that I'd been in Japan at the time of the service.

It also occurred to me that there probably wouldn't be any need to be all that formal, since the only older people likely to be there were Oharu-baasan and my older brother and his wife—meaning that most of the people would be younger than me.

"How long will it take? I'm meeting a painter friend of mine that evening at a loft near Harumi Futo Park on Tokyo Bay."

"It shouldn't take the *bonze* all that long to chant the sutra. Temples are just like businesses these days, and they've got it all figured out. If they spend too long on each service, they can't do as much business. Anyway, after he's done, I suppose we'll all go somewhere to eat. If it starts at one I should think everything should be over by five, wouldn't it? You know, you have to take along money in a *okumotsu ryo* envelope as an offering."

"Huh? What in the world is that for?" I'd forgotten the mechanics of these traditional Japanese ceremonies, but none-theless, I felt a familiar resentment welling up over the way they always involved handing over envelopes stuffed with money.

"To cover the cost of the *bonze* and the meal. That's par for the course for a *hoji*."

"Who do you give it to?"

"I'll take care of that for you."

"How much do people give?"

"Well, for you, I'd say about ¥20,000."

"What?" Without thinking, I let my shock escape my lips. The yen is strong right now, so ¥20,000 would be about $180.00. That's a lot of money for someone like me who lives in Los Angeles. Prices in Tokyo are about triple what they are in the States, so most people here also have higher incomes as well, and I suppose to them, this is no big deal. "Do different people pay different amounts?"

"Sure. Someone like me has to pay more," said my mother as she picked up her teacup.

In America, the family putting on the funeral pays for every-thing. Of course, that may add up to a lot of money, but there's only the funeral to pay for, not multiple *hoji* memorial services on top of it. And people who can't afford a big funeral just have a simple gathering and serve tea in their homes or let friends handle the arrangements.

But in Japan after someone dies, the expenses don't end with the funeral; you've also got to have *hoji* services on various anni-versaries of the death. (I personally believe this system was devel-oped for the sole purpose of allowing temples to make money. And since religious organizations are totally exempt from taxes on their income, it's a clean take for the Buddhist priests!)

Then there's the huge amounts of money given as *koden* offerings to the departed soul—does all of that go to the funeral directors and the temple? If that's really where the money is going, I would think it would be better to do like people often do in America, and say that in lieu of flowers, offerings should be sent to such and such a hospital or institution or research lab in the name of the departed soul. To people coming from another country, Japan's weddings, funerals and other ceremonial occasions must be as hard to grasp as a cloud.

"Remember last year when I was in Japan—it was just at New Year's time, right?" I reminded my mother. "When we were watching TV—it was so obvious that this was the season for the shrines and temples to make money that it was just disgusting! What's worse, some of them were even bald-faced enough to call themselves corporations and pay for TV commercials. I couldn't believe how much New Year in Japan had changed in the twenty-five years I'd been away. According to the newspaper, a record number of people went to the shrines and temples that year, but I wonder: didn't any of those people feel even a little bit of a contradiction in shrines and temples calling themselves corporations? Are they all so dense that they don't know what religion really is?"

"Auntie Ikuyo's family put on a big funeral for her. You know, Buddhism is really *yayakoshii*—with *hojis* and all sorts of stuff even after you die."

"*Homma ya*," I agreed. "Every time I come back to Japan, I see lots of people wearing mourning clothes milling around in train stations and it always seems like a lot of people die in this country, but I suppose it's just because everybody—even people who aren't related to the deceased—wears black to all these ceremonies. In America, only people in the family of the departed wear black clothes or a black armband, so other people don't stand out so much."

To my delight, we'd arrived at what seemed like the perfect opportunity for me to ask about something that I'd been concerned about for a while now. You see, some time earlier, my brother and sister had consulted me about what to do for a funeral if something ever happened to Oharu-baasan. My family is Buddhist on both my father's and mother's sides, with Oharu-baasan being the only one who broke with family tradition and became a Christian. Since she had been baptized as a Christian when she was young, we all felt that we could not have the same kind of funeral for her as we did for the rest of the family. None of the rest of us—that is, her children—have been baptized, although we were all sent to Sunday school.

"Obaachan, you wouldn't think of having a Buddhist funeral, would you?" I asked. "Since you were baptized and all. The Christian way is so much simpler, with no *koden* monetary offerings or memorial services on the anniversary of people's death. Wouldn't it be a good idea to decide on what you'd like now?"

"*So ya ne*," she mused. "I haven't been to church in a long time. And on top of that, I was baptized in Osaka, not here."

"Well, if that's a problem, I have a couple of friends in Tokyo who are Christians—they could look for a church near your retirement home. Then you could go to church on Sundays and get to know the minister, and then ask to be taken care of when the time comes. If nothing was settled in advance, we'd all have a hard time figuring out what to do on the spur of the moment. Deciding what to do now would be a kind of 'parental piety,' you know—fulfilling your duty to your children," I reasoned.

"Yesss!" I thought. "I should get a medal for that! I'll have to brag about this to Yoshio and Chii-chan" (my younger sister, Chizu).

"I'm a Congregationalist, you know. I went to that church that was in the Tosabori area of Osaka," said Oharu-baasan, sipping her tea as she stared out into space.

"Err, there's some *yokan* red bean jelly from Toraya here," I interjected, remembering some sweets from the famous Japanese confectionery that I'd received as a gift. "This should be all right even with those teeth of yours." I cut the firm rectangular block of jelly with a knife, arranged some on a small plate and put it on the table.

"The missionary at that church had been in Japan for a long time, and his Japanese was pretty good, but sometimes his pronunciation was funny. Instead of saying '*oshi ire wo shimete kudasai*,' he'd say '*oshiri wo shimete kudasai*,'" she explained, prolonging the first *I* and changing the *E* sound to an *I* (which meant that instead of asking you to close the sliding doors on Japanese-style closets, he seemed to be telling you to "close your rear end"). "Everyone there had the hardest time trying not to laugh at him."

"I've heard that story dozens of times," I sighed.

But as she cut the *yokan* jelly I'd put out for her with her small fork and put it into her mouth, she continued reminiscing. "Back then, I went to the missionary's house a lot. I learned how to crochet lace, and cook, and other things there. Without those lessons, I wouldn't have known how to knit sweaters for you guys, or make cabbage rolls or caramel, either. Remember how the smell of butter filled the house? Those were good times." As she spoke, she lifted her face, deeply chiseled with wrinkles, as if to gaze out into the distance, and peered out of the window on the right. All that was out there was the cement wall of the neighboring apartment, which had been spray-painted creamy white.

"So, about Sunday: where's the temple?" I asked.

"It's somewhere just outside of Kamakura. I'm going with Yoshio in his car, and you could meet us at his place. Sadao will probably be coming, too, I should think."

I'd completely forgotten about Uncle Sadao up until that point. He's my mother's brother, and I really liked him when I was a child. "How's he doing? How old is he now?" I asked.

"Eighty, I guess. I think he's doing all right."

3

I went into the kitchen and started preparing dinner. I don't
know how much my son cooks, but he has an incredible array
of spices lined up next to the window. Unfortunately, there
wouldn't be much of a chance for me to test them out tonight,
since at my mother's request, dinner was going to be a Japanese-
style one-pot *nabe* meal.

The fish in America are all quite large, so, being back in
Japan, I'd gone to a fish shop in hopes of getting some nice
medium-size fish. Unfortunately, the seafood in Tokyo just isn't
as fresh as that in the Kansai area, so I ended up pacing back
and forth in front of the store for quite some time. Still, if I
hadn't bought any fish just because their stocks weren't very
fresh, there would have been nothing for me to buy, so I finally
lowered my standards and picked something out.

Happily, the big daikon radish I got was much juicier than
anything you could get in America. As I grated it on a metal
grater, I recalled the time years ago when I was living in New
York just after I got married, and, unable to find a daikon, I
bought regular American radishes and had to grate at least
twenty to be able to make a reasonable amount of *daikon oroshi*.
Now, as I worked, I listened to my elderly mother tell me stories

about her retirement home that I'd already heard many times before. Then during dinner, I had to listen to the story about the missionary that she'd just recounted, and when I said that I'd already heard it, she changed the subject to her dentist.

I'm amazed at how her voice holds out. Personally, I become hoarse if I speak for very long, but my mother seems to pick up steam as she talks, and she rattles on for so long without a break that she almost wears me out. There are times when I wonder if this isn't a sign of the onset of senility. You know how people sometimes run loose around town when they start to lose their minds—well, I worry that in my mother's case, that kind of manic energy has just been channeled into verbal output. On the other hand, it occurs to me that most of the time she is alone in her room in the retirement home and the only time she talks all day is when she's in the dining hall, so perhaps it's inevitable that she talks so much when she has the chance. I feel sorry for her then, though I keep a very close eye on her.

After dinner, the two of us sat down on the sofa in the living room to relax.

"You know," said my mother, "I read something recently in a magazine—was it *Pumpkin* or *Lettuce* or *Croissant*—I forget . . ."

"What are you talking about?" I asked, totally taken aback. "Those are all names of food—they're not magazines!" I became even more worried that she was becoming senile.

"They are too magazines," she said matter-of-factly.

"You can't let yourself go like this!" I cried. Having been away from Japan for so long, I had no idea that these English labels for different types of food really *were* the names of women's magazines.

Suddenly, I got an idea about how I could make my senile old mother shut up: television. Why didn't I think of that earlier? So I quickly turned on the TV—to NHK, Japan's public broadcasting network. However, the picture was spinning like a top, and I couldn't figure out how to stop it. Thinking that my mother's mental condition might become even worse if she looked at a picture like that, I hurriedly changed channels and was relieved to find that the image stayed still this time.

A female reporter was talking about Rie Miyazawa and the screen showed an almost-nude young woman who looked like a starlet or something like that. I thought she might be the granddaughter of Prime Minister Miyazawa, and perhaps that was why her posing for nude photographs was seen as problematic. I changed channels again. The picture didn't spin, but again, it was a shot of the beautiful Rie Miyazawa standing in the nude. I turned the channel knob again. Same thing. It seemed like this TV only had two channels: the spinning NHK or the one showing Rie Miyzawa. As I was asking myself whether I should have Oharu-baasan look at pictures of a naked woman, she quickly said, "I don't watch anything but NHK. I have trouble finding it when I go to Chizu's house, though, because the channel numbers are different in Kansai—it's really a pain."

"Yes, but, John doesn't have cable, so the picture on NHK spins, and no matter how many times I turn the channel knob, the only other thing I get is pictures of a naked woman, so I guess this channel is all we can get. You'll just have to put up with it."

"Ahh. That's a young actress called Rie Miyazawa. She's really caused a big fuss, hasn't she? These days, the only thing all the newspapers and TV channels talk about is her."

"Oh? Is she the granddaughter of Prime Minister Miyazawa?"

"What are you talking about? She's a 'half,' isn't she—like John."

"Don't call people like that 'half.' They're 'doubles.' They have two cultures. Anyway, doesn't Prime Minister Miyazawa have a grandchild like John? His daughter is in an international marriage, isn't she?"

"That may be, but this is not his granddaughter. Anyway, I wonder what it is with this TV. When I stayed here before, the picture was spinning, and I told John about it, but he said, 'Grandma, it's just your eyes.' He insisted that there was nothing wrong with the image. He likes to tease people, that boy."

4

It was now Sunday, two days after Oharu-baasan went home. To go to Auntie Ikuyo's *hoji* at the temple on the outskirts of Kamakura, I had put on a pair of gray wool slacks and a white wool turtleneck sweater, over which I had on a raincoat. To make sure that my feet wouldn't get cold, I had put on wool socks and sneakers with thick soles. It can get chilly in November in Japan, and especially in the suburbs, it's a lot colder than it is in the middle of Tokyo. Also, when you're coming from sunny Southern California, these temperatures feel even colder. Besides, I thought, temples are always cold, empty places. I had three more weeks in this country, so I'd be in a real fix if I caught a cold.

It was a clear, fine fall day. When I got to my brother's house in Suginami Ward, Oharu-baasan was already there, and it was decided that my nephew would drive us to Kamakura. My mother and my brother's plump wife Nobuko were both properly dressed in black suits that looked like uniforms. Seeing that, I remarked, in a puzzled tone, "Wow. You're both wearing black—like it's a funeral."

In Southern California, mourners who are not members of the family wear clothing of all colors, even at funerals. A painter friend of mine once wore a red dress to the funeral of another painter.

"These days everyone wears fairly formal clothing, even to *hojis*. But I suppose you wouldn't know that because you haven't lived here for so long, Megumi. People in Japan have become extravagant, haven't they? Auntie Ikuyo's funeral was especially lavish. Her son Yuichi is a bigwig at M Trading Company, and I suppose they had to consider how it would reflect on the business, too. A lot of people from the corporation came to help out. I should have called you yesterday to tell you what to wear, shouldn't I?"

"Even if you had told me ahead of time, there would have been nothing I could have done—I didn't bring anything like that along . . . Anyway, it'll probably get cold in the evening."

Nobuko, whose hair was still black even though she was two years older than me, looked at me with a slightly pitying expression on her long face.

When we reached the temple and got out of the car, we saw two bulldozers going back and forth, leveling the ground in the vacant lot next to the temple parking lot. I wondered what they were making. It could have been a cemetery, or maybe they were just enlarging the parking lot, but in my mind, temples and bulldozers do not go together, so the combination was jarring. I wondered if they were doing it to rake in more money. Was this temple a corporation too?

Off to our right, at the top of a tall stone stairway, stood a splendid, brand-spanking-new temple gate. There must have been at least fifty steps. Wondering whether my poor old mother could possibly climb them, my heart sank for a moment, but Nobuko stepped in and said, "Megumi, you take Mother's left arm and I'll take her right and we'll go up like that." Hoisting her up in that fashion, the two of us managed to get her up the stone stairs while my brother and nephew paid us no mind. I think in America, the men would have handled this. No matter how bad their hearts are or even if their legs are somewhat bad, the men over there do this kind of thing. I don't know which is better. I guess the younger, stronger people should do it, regardless of their sex.

"What sect does this temple belong to? It's really something, isn't it?" I said between gasps for air as we panted our way up the stairs. I figured it probably belonged to the Jodo Shinshu sect.

"This . . . is . . . Zen . . . a . . . Zen . . . temple," stated Oharu-baasan as she gasped for breath.

"Ohh?" I said, letting out a long breath while I stopped for a moment—which meant that the other two stopped, too.

The Zen temples that I knew of were ones like Kokedera Moss Temple, the rock garden temple Ryoanji and other old temples that I had seen on sightseeing trips I made while I was a student at Kyoto University of Arts. That was before the so-called economic "bubble" years, so the image of Zen entrenched in my mind was simplicity itself, almost completely cut off from the material world, with even the food being only enough to keep a soul one step from starvation.

This image derives from my memory of one night while David and I were living in Kyoto after we got married, when a young American Zen trainee showed up at our door and begged us to give him something to eat. He had dropped out of college in his longing to follow the Zen path and had been training at a temple in Kyoto, but he ended up fleeing the compound under the cover of night. He was so emaciated he looked like one of the survivors of the Nazi concentration camp at Auschwitz. And how he did eat! In one sitting, he cleaned us out of all the food we had in the house. He consumed what the two of us could have lived on for three days. Declaring that he would not go back to the Zen temple, he stayed with us for a month before he returned to America.

Inside the temple gate in Kamakura, there was a large cluster of small maple trees ablaze with fall colors. Looking at them, I was reminded of how many shades of autumn colors there are, ranging from gold to vermilion and on to rust red. In contrast to the impressive scale of the fall leaves in the New England area of the United States, where the colored leaves of the large maple trees completely cover the ground like huge flames at your feet, these Japanese maples displayed a more delicate brilliance; clearly set off against the white of the newly plastered wall behind them, they added cheer to their surroundings.

After walking the pathway of granite slabs dappled by the shadows of the maple leaves, we arrived at the large, impressive entranceway to the temple.

There we took off our shoes. I was embarrassed to see how the slightly dirty white of my sneakers stood out among all the shiny black shoes of the other guests, but I just stepped into one of the pairs of slippers lined up in the entranceway and headed off down a long hallway in the direction of an arrow pointing the way to the waiting room. Going out onto the *engawa* porch that ran along the outside of the building, I saw an expansive, newly landscaped Japanese garden with rocks and sand on the right, and was quite captivated by it until I heard Nobuko call out to me from my left. "Here," she indicated, as she knelt in front of a set of *shoji* sliding doors that smelled of new wood.

Inside, the sliding paper *fusuma* doors that normally separated two adjoining rooms had been removed to create a waiting room that must have been a full forty tatami mats in size. A large number of people were already gathered there, but I recognized only the round smiling face of Auntie Ikuyo's eldest son, Yuichi. He had just graduated from college when I was living in Japan, so I could figure out who he was, but Auntie Ikuyo's other children were all much younger than me, so I had never even met them.

When Yuichi saw me, he came over to greet me. "Megumi-san, you're back over here now? It's really been a long time, hasn't it? It must be thirty years since the last time I saw you. I haven't seen you since around the time I was recruited by my company and then graduated from college."

"Is that right? Now that you mention it, it must have been the very same year that I went to America. But look at you now—you've turned into a middle-aged salaryman!"

Yuichi laughed. "You're looking very dashing. But yes, I'm getting close to retirement age now. How many years has it been since you went to America?"

"Hmm. This is 1992—so it's been thirty years."

"But I've forgotten to give you a formal greeting. Thank you so much for taking time out of your busy schedule to join us today. I'm sure that my late mother is delighted that you came even though it was such a long distance."

I followed Yuichi's lead and switched into the formulaic phrases used on such occasions: "Please excuse me for being so remiss as to miss her funeral."

"You are too polite. It is I who must apologize. I lived in London for five years—I was sent by my company—and while I was there, I went to Atlanta on business two times, but I was not able to make it out to the West Coast to see you. I'm sorry I didn't visit you." Yuichi's long years of work at a trading company had obviously helped him become quite the diplomat.

Switching back to Kansai-ben, I asked, "What took you to Atlanta?"

"Investment business. One of the top people in the company

told me that such and such a company had bought a certain kind of building, so I should buy something at least that good so that we didn't get left behind. So I was buying land and stuff. In America and Europe."

"Ah, *that* kind of investment. In Los Angeles, too, up until about two years ago, Japanese companies were buying up properties right and left. Americans were saying that they were driving up house prices and were really upset by it. They said that usually, the Japanese companies didn't bargain at all when they bought real estate, so naturally, the prices went up. Realtors were ecstatic, though. 'It's so easy with Japanese buyers,' they'd say; 'they don't bargain.' Still, you wonder if it was really all right for people to make purchases like that. Just because land prices here in Japan are sky high, that doesn't give them the right to push them up there, too!"

"Megumi-san, that's really harsh! We didn't do anything like that," Yuichi protested in his strong Osaka accent. "We're Kansai-ites, and our company was originally from Kansai, too. So naturally we drive a tough bargain, even overseas—that's what they mean in English by the word 'negotiation,' isn't it?"

I was reminded of a time when David and I had lunch with some friends of his in a restaurant in New York. One of his friends who worked for the New York Times arrived late, and as soon as he sat down, his face took on a sour expression as he announced in a strained voice, "I hear that Mitsubishi bought Rockefeller Center!"

I'll never forget how they all—with the exception of David—reacted. "What? Didn't they used to make Zero fighter planes? What is this world coming to?"

No one would have reacted like that if a Dutch or British company had bought that building. First of all, it wouldn't even have been reported in the newspapers. But if a Japanese company buys such a landmark, they write about it as if it's a serious concern.

Afterward, David said their reaction was foolish, especially since they weren't financiers. He said that capitalists all over the world have a sense of solidarity with each other. They have nothing to do with us.

Still, although I am in no way connected to Mitsubishi and have no need to defend them, I was the only Japanese person there that day, and I was really shocked by their reaction. At the time, I thought Mitsubishi had no need to buy such a famous building just to show off to its Japanese competitors, and what it really was purchasing was antipathy. Americans still feel the effects of World War II, and, come to think of it, so do Japanese people of my generation. The younger generation shake their heads at us because even now, we fear war—we start to tremble just at the sound of the word "bomb" and are always trying to economize. But I guess that's just inevitable.

Still thinking about that incident, I said to Yuichi, "I think that at some point, Japanese companies will be done in by the old eastern establishment—the Rockefellers or the Morgans or some other group like that. The Japanese don't do their homework; they just go after brand names. They're seen as easy marks and I can't help but think they're being conned. The old American companies have been in international trade for a long time, and they really know the ropes. I think the Japanese companies are in an especially precarious situation, because in Japan, they were in cahoots with the Ministry of Finance and the banks when they raised land prices."

Of all the relatives who were gathered for the ceremony, Yuichi was probably the one who knew the most about things outside of Japan, so I just didn't seem to be able to stop myself from spewing out what I'd been thinking.

Yuichi, on the other hand, seemed to have heard quite enough on that subject, for he asked, "How long are you going to be here this time?"

"Another three weeks."

Then Nobuko, who looked like she was wondering how long we would continue on with this pointless conversation, came over to exchange greetings with Yuichi.

Once that was done, Nobuko said she'd introduce me to everyone. She began with someone very close to us: a woman in her early fifties who looked like a Kyoto doll sitting primly in an expensively tailored black suit with pearl earrings and a pearl necklace.

"Why, Mayumi-san. It's been a long time. Thank you for inviting us today," Nobuko said in very polite, formulaic Japanese. "It's been two years already, hasn't it? How time flies. How has everyone been since then? Is your family all in good health? Also, let me say that I'm very grateful to you for always, always sending us seasonal gifts. We're so beholden to you. From now on, please do not put yourself to so much trouble on our account." As she delivered this greeting in very polite Japanese, Nobuko's carefully painted eyebrows rose and fell while she knelt and made a formal bow, virtually rubbing her forehead on the tatami mat. Then she hurriedly opened her handbag and took out a neatly folded white linen handkerchief and put it to her nose as she let out a tiny sneeze. She probably had breathed in some dust from the tatami.

Nobuko then straightened her back and, turning back toward me, pointed in my direction with her left hand and said, "Errr . . . this is my sister-in-law Megumi. You've never met her, have you? Megumi, this is Yuichi's wife, Mayumi."

"How do you do," we both said. It seemed that she was also from the Kansai area. I got the feeling that this gathering was a clear demonstration of the results of the Japanese government's centralization policies. Except for the children, everyone here was speaking Kansai-ben.

I bowed clumsily. It had been many years since the last time I had sat properly with my legs tucked under me Japanese style in slacks on tatami, so as I braced myself with my hands on the reed matting, my behind wobbled in midair. 'I shouldn't have come,' I thought, keenly regretting having agreed to attend the ceremony as I squirmed on the tatami.

Just then, Nobuko decided to explain my outfit to Mayumi. "Megumi is just visiting and didn't have anything appropriate to wear along with her. Also, she's not used to the climate here anymore, so that's why she looks like this. She's on the road, so please forgive her disrespectful appearance."

"No one would have noticed if you hadn't said anything," I thought as Mayumi casually looked over my clothes. But now that I thought of it, I wondered whether it was my clothing that Yuichi had been referring to earlier when he'd said, "You're looking very dashing." I got flustered. "I'm an adult," I thought, "so other people shouldn't have to go around explaining my actions and appearance for me. Japan is a picky place. I can't stand it."

My appearance shouldn't have made any difference, but somehow, it seemed like there were secret rules. Even the amount of money to give is decided by these secret rules in this country, so when I come back from overseas, I'm like a child, needing everything patiently explained to me.

5

The alcove in the waiting room—into which Oharu-baasan had been squinting for some time now—held a large Korean white porcelain urn with an arrangement of pine branches and red camelia blossoms, while behind that hung a scroll depicting monkeys painted by the pre-war Kyoto artist Hashimoto Kansetsu. The decorative shelf held an ostentatious array, which included a valuable gold lacquerware box for a calligraphy inkstone, a crystal vase and a colorful pottery figure of a woman made in the Tang Sancai style, all of which combined made me feel like I had come to the home of a nouveau riche family.

"Wow, this is really something!" enthused my mother. Then she sighed and added, "We had things like this, too, but I couldn't get them into my room at the retirement home, so I gave them all away."

"What? To whom?"

"To Yoshio's family, and Chizu's."

"Oh?"

I realized at that moment that I hadn't inherited any of those family treasures. You lose out in all sorts of ways when you live outside the country. It had been clear from my mother's explanation of the expected amounts for monetary offerings the other day that people base their calculations on the assumption that the giver will be attending the event (and therefore include the cost of the meal in the amount). This meant that for weddings, say, it was not necessary for someone like me, who wouldn't be going to the ceremony, to follow my brother and sister's advice and give the same amount as they did. Yet no one had ever explained that to me, so I had always done what they said and therefore had been giving too much. Now I kind of understand why foreign governments get angry at Japan and say it's not fair. It seems strange to me that the people on the receiving end don't see that they're not treating people who live outside the country equally . . . but what the heck—both David and I dislike having lots of things lying around, so we've gotten by without raising a fuss about this kind of treatment.

A Japanese friend living in Los Angeles once let it slip out that even though she had sent money to congratulate her nieces and nephews when they started college, no one had sent anything when her daughter started university. She sighed, "We're like people who have been abandoned by their own country."

6

I suddenly realized that my younger sister Chizu had not come to the ceremony.

Chizu lives near Shukugawa Station on the Hankyu Line between Osaka and Kobe, on the side of the station that rises up towards the mountains. She's fifty years old now, and her husband, who's a physics professor at K. University, is about fifty-five. The two of them met and fell in love when they were students at K. University, but they married late. Her husband's name is Tatsuo; he's very handsome but disgustingly arrogant—always looking down at other people. It's enough to make one wonder how in the world Chizu could have fallen in love with him. I sometimes think my sister must have been deluded, but of course, no one really knows what goes on in a marriage. I imagine some people are happy as long as their spouse looks attractive.

And I suppose they probably criticize all sorts of things about David and me. First of all, they may wonder how we could possibly live together when we can only understand about half of what the other person is saying. For my part, I make excuses, telling myself that even if you only understand half of the other person's words, that's not much of a barrier to a good sex life.

Likes and dislikes are all instinctive —the result of DNA.

"Oh, lovely. Touch there. Oh, yes. Oh, wonderful! More! More! Oh, darling, you are wonderful! Sweetheart. Ah . . . Ah . . . Nice. Nice."

That's all you need at first. By the time children arrive on the scene, you'll be able to speak to each other.

But back to Chizu and Tatsuo: They have two children. The older one, a boy named Ichiro, is probably a senior in high school now. The younger one is a girl who's probably in her first year of high school—but I'm not sure, as I don't keep track of the age of other people's children.

I whispered to my mother, who was sitting next to me, "Chizu isn't here, is she?"

"Chizu—yes—I got a call from her this morning, and she said that something had come up so she couldn't come today. I have no idea what it is—she said she'd explain later and hung up."

"Oh?"

Then suddenly Uncle Sadao came over to us. His face had become round and strangely cute—not at all like the impressive manner he displayed years ago when he was still working in the Daimaru Department Store.

"Haru-nei-chan. How you doin'?" he called out, his Osaka origins clearly evident in his wording.

I was surprised to hear my uncle refer to my mother as "Haru-nei-chan"—a combination of her name plus an affectionate term for one's older sister. It seemed odd that even at such a ripe old age, he would still refer to her in the same way he had when he was a little child.

"My, my—long time no see. How's it goin'?" she responded.

"Well . . . I'm living in Nagoya now."

"What? Why would you live somewhere like that?" my mother said in a high-pitched voice, opening her wrinkled eyes wide as she looked at Uncle Sadao in surprise.

"Huh? I'm renting an apartment near Kazuo's place," he explained—Kazuo being his eldest son.

"You sold your house in Osaka?"

"No. Shizue's living there."

"What in the world is going on?"

Uncle Sadao lowered his eyes and said in a small, weak voice, "We decided to separate. I can't stand her anymore."

"Ooh! That's terrible! I have no idea what happened, of course. What's Shizue living on?" My mother's face had gradually stiffened.

"I gave her the house and my whole pension. I should still be able to get a job. It's easier this way. Kazuo's wife says, 'I'm willing to take care of you, father, but I couldn't stand taking care of mother.'"

"Sada-chan," my mother said, referring to Uncle Sadao in the same way she had when he was a little boy, "how old are you now?"

"I'll be eighty next month."

"Someone'll hire you when you're eighty?"

"Hmm. Well, I'll manage somehow."

I hadn't greeted my uncle yet, but there had been no opening for me, so I thought I'd hold back for a while yet and was just listening to the two of them in silence. Actually, I was surprised. You often hear about the new trend of people getting divorced later in life in Japan, but in most cases, it's around the time people retire—in their sixties. I was dumbfounded to learn that I had an elderly relative who had separated from his wife when he was pushing eighty. In America, it's fairly common for couples in their eighties to just live together without getting married because financially it makes more sense, as they get twice as much social security that way, but Uncle Sadao's situation was something quite different.

It's impossible to see inside a marriage, but for people to reach a point where they want to throw everything away and split up after reaching their eighties, they must have built up an awful lot of animosity over the years. I thought people became less sensitive as they got older, so they let little things pass. That's why even if you dislike your spouse somewhat and have an argument, the next day, you forget all about it and act as if nothing happened. At least, that's what I thought based on my own experience, so I was surprised to find that this wasn't true for everyone.

I don't know how much longer I have to live, but I suppose it's possible that sometime during the next twenty years or so it may happen that my partner and I will no longer get along at all. What if your partner becomes senile but at first you don't realize that that's what's happening, so you argue and get angry at them? I guess that could happen if you didn't notice they were having neurological problems, and you could end up being at odds with the other person for a long time. There must be at least some of Uncle Sadao's genes in me, so I suppose it would be possible for me to do this kind of thing, too. When I realized that, my heart skipped a beat.

After that, I formally greeted Uncle Sadao, and in the joy of seeing each other again after eight years, we talked about how I'd been getting on and many other things. However, since his situation was so totally removed from anything I'd imagined, I ended up not being able to talk very openly with him.

After my uncle had returned to the other side of the room, I said to Oharu-baasan, "Even in this kind of situation, how can Uncle Sadao talk about working at his age? And even if he did give Auntie his pension and their house, didn't he have any other assets? You, Grandma, and Auntie Ikuyo, too—didn't you all get equal shares of Grandpa Gensaku's estate when he died? His eldest son—our late uncle who lived in Tosabori—sure had an opulent lifestyle anyway."

"Well, there's the rub. Grandpa Gensaku died just after the war ended—before the new constitution was in place, so the eldest son got everything. Uncle Sadao didn't get anything. Of course, neither did us girls."

"Well, that's terrible, isn't it? I can't quite understand our dead uncle—didn't he ever feel that he should give you all a little?"

"Ahh, there's nothing we can do about it now. Anyway, Sadao's younger son, Shimpei, who lives in Fukuoka, seems to be close to Chizu's son, Ichiro. Last summer vacation, Ichiro happened to go down there and got Shimpei to let him work in his restaurant, and they liked each other, so he's planning on going down there again."

"Uncle Sadao's son has a restaurant? I didn't know he liked cooking. Wow. I didn't think that we had that kind of thing in our blood. Especially judging from you, Grandma."

"What're you saying? When I had the ingredients, I made delicious food, didn't I? It's just that during the war, there was nothing to cook with, so I started to hate cooking."

"Wait a minute. I saw something in the paper yesterday about Fukuoka—it seems there are a lot of *yakuza* there. There was a shoot-out in Fukuoka, wasn't there? If you've got a restaurant, those *yakuza* guys are really picky about whose turf it's on, aren't they?"

"You don't say? I had no idea." Oharu-baasan's face suddenly darkened.

7

The waiting room had filled up with lots of relatives whom I'd never seen before and was rather noisy. Nobuko introduced me to all sorts of people, but since it's hard to attach names to faces in such a short time, I gave up trying to remember them. The children of my young cousins were junior high school students or younger.

I was starting to feel dizzy because the gas heater next to me was throwing off so much heat, but just then, Yuichi announced that it was time to go in to the main building of the temple. I had been kneeling in the formal position with my legs folded under me, so they hurt quite a bit when I stood up and I ended up dragging them along as I followed the line of people going into the hall for the Buddhist service.

The wooden floor of the hall was polished to a black sheen that brought back fond memories of the old kitchen of our house in Tezukayama in Osaka.

In the front of the room, there was a large gold Buddha on a dais. All religions use gold as a symbol of authority, don't they? I wonder if people equate the high price of gold with the strength of authority, thinking that the more gold they use, the more powerful their religion will appear.

In front of the Buddha, lying on the floor on both sides of the hall were two large groups of *zabuton* cushions. They were arranged with an equal number on either side, positioned so that the people attending the ceremony would sit facing each other. This meant that we were to supposed sit on the *zabuton*, but I knew that would be really hard on me, since I had not done anything like that in thirty years and my body was just not that flexible anymore. Earlier, I had had trouble sitting in the waiting room and that was on tatami mats; this was on a wood floor, which would be even harder. There was no heater here, either, so we would get chilled.

"This is bad," I was thinking, when I happened to glance back and what did I see but a large number of cylindrical stools lined up along the wall; they were about twenty centimeters in diameter and twenty-five centimeters high and were covered in blue velvet. How thoughtful! These days Westerners also probably come to the temple, so they're all prepared for them! Not attempting to hide my joy at this marvelous discovery, I stood up and rushed over to where the stools were, and, picking one up, returned to my place; I folded my cushion in two and pushed it aside, then put down the stool and sat on it. I felt strange because I was little higher up than everyone else.

No sooner was I seated than Yuichi—who was sitting in the group on the other side of the hall—spotted me and said, "Megumi, that looks really comfortable. I believe I will follow your lead."

He stood up and came over to where the stools were, took one, then went back to his place. Almost immediately, other participants, apparently thinking the same thing, got up one after the next and took stools for themselves. Eventually, my nephew brought one for Oharu-baasan. These days, even in

Japan, people tend to sit on chairs rather than on the floor, so everyone seemed delighted with the stools; using them meant that even if the sutra chanting went on for a long time, the participants could sit through the ceremony without their legs going to sleep.

A tall Buddhist priest who appeared to be about fifty-five years old entered and sat on a cushion placed in the empty space in the center of the hall. He wore a purple robe with a gold brocade priest's stole over his shoulders. Looking out at the people gathered for the service, the *bonze* must have noticed that something was strange—everyone was looking down at him—for he muttered,

"Er . . . the blue things you all are sitting on are used for Zen meditation."

We all looked at each other with awkward expressions on our faces as we suppressed the urge to laugh, but not a single person made a move to return their stool. I wonder if the *bonze* thought we would put them away if he made a comment like that? Before the war, everyone would have. Japan has changed a little, I thought. I was the one who had started this, but no matter what anyone said to me—even if everyone else put their stool back—I figured that using a stool would be better than not being able to stand up later on because my legs had fallen asleep, so I had not the slightest intention of putting mine away.

Since no one looked like they were going to move, the *bonze* started reading a sutra. Our behavior may even have been unsettling enough to cause him to slip up in his chanting. But even if he had made a mistake, not a single person there would have noticed. With the exception of Oharu-baasan, they were all young, and she—the oldest and most likely to complain—was a Christian, so she probably wouldn't have picked it up either.

I almost never think about religion, but it's inevitable when you come to a place like this. While I was listening to the sutra, I was thinking about how gods and war go together. In World War II, Americans believed they were fighting a holy war under the Christian god, yet they put Japanese Americans in relocation camps even though they were American citizens. They also dropped atomic bombs on Hiroshima and Nagasaki and then falsely claimed that the bombs had saved the lives of a million American soldiers.

In Japan, people believed that a *kamikaze* divine wind would arise to protect them, and that the Emperor was a living god. For the sake of that god, millions of the country's young men were forced to repeatedly sing an ode to death:

> If I go to the sea, I shall become a brine-sodden corpse
> If I go to the mountains, my carcass shall sprout grass
> I shall die in your environs, O great one,
> And never look back.

For the sake of that god, millions of Japan's young men were brainwashed with the Bushido ideals espoused in the eighteenth-century tome *Hagakure*, which taught that the way of the samurai is found in death. For the sake of that god, millions of Japan's young men were sent off to die. Needless to say, those young men also killed untold numbers of people throughout Asia. What was Buddhism doing then? Entangled with Shintoism, it did not oppose the war. Buddhists were busy praying for fortune in the war effort and burying tens of thousands of the dead. I suppose you could say that their business was flourishing. Religion always joins forces with authority.

In Europe, Germany's Hitler claimed that the Aryans—that

is, the white Christians—were the master race and tried to root out what he called an inferior race—the Jewish people—by killing six million of them. Even though Christianity sprang from Judaism and both religions believe in the God Jehovah. He also killed millions more communists, Gypsies and the mentally disabled.

Moreover, in ancient times, Japan persecuted Christians, while in Europe, Christians—who had been whipped into a frenzy of mob violence—killed large numbers of unusual women, especially intelligent ones, who had been labeled witches, as well as heretics and Jews, who were seen as heathens. All this is enough to make me shudder when I hear the word religion.

People tend to think that people who are devoted to a religion are good, but in all societies, there are those who do evil in the name of their faith and use their "piety" as a smoke screen. Granted, the ranks of the religious include some amazing souls. But the founding members of the antinuclear movement were not religious, were they? They were atheists like Bertrand Russell, Linus Pauling, and Jean-Paul Sartre.

The *bonze* was facing the Buddha's dais, chanting the sutra in a sleepy-sounding voice.

Since my son Ken is mentally disabled, I have read a lot of books about the brain, and I've begun to think that if there ever comes a time when the functioning of brain cells is fully understood, the raison d'être for things like religions and philosophy may well disappear. I wonder if experiences like hearing God reveal himself during meditation or reaching the state of enlightenment or suddenly getting flashes of inspiration might just be due to the functioning of the synapses connecting nerve cells. I suspect that since ancient times, the working of the brain has been a mystery, and that's why religions and philosophy developed. Kant's theory of the power of imagination is a good example of this.

All the same, compared to philosophers, who tend to be bad at making money, I suppose religionists are smart: They make money without having any capital to start with. If Ken had lived in ancient times, he may have been worshipped as the god of anger or the thunder deity. As a woman, I might even have been revered like the Virgin Mary, or in the worst-case scenario, burned at the stake as a witch.

Consider the *bonze* at the front of the hall—in his fluttery purple robe and gold embroidered stole that looks like something that belongs in a fashion show. If a normal person walked down the street looking like that, everyone would laugh.

Suddenly I came out of my reverie and noticed that the chanting had stopped. I was amazed at how quickly the sutra had been completed. There had hardly even been time for my legs to fall asleep.

8

Two days after the *hoji*, before I'd even had breakfast, I got a phone call from my sister-in-law Nobuko.

"Megumi, I don't understand this at all, but just now your mother called and in a frantic voice said she was setting out for Kyushu. When I asked her if she was going to a spa—Beppu perhaps—she said she was going to Fukuoka. Then I asked what she was going to do there, and she said that Chizu's boy Ichiro ran away from home and it would be awful if he joined the *yakuza*. Of all her grandchildren, Ichiro is the one she's most concerned about."

"What does running away from home have to do with the *yakuza*?"

"I don't know. Grandma is always like this. She's always making leaps in logic."

"Why did Ichiro run away?"

"Apparently Tatsuo got really angry at Ichiro and hit him on the head. I guess Ichiro said he wouldn't go to college—that these days, there's nothing good about going. And of course Tatsuo is teaching at a prestigious national university. I suppose he wanted to keep up appearances in front of his colleagues, too; he may have thought that it would look bad if the son of a college professor—and a famous one at that—didn't even go to college, so they had a big fight. And apparently, this wasn't the first time."

"What was Chizu doing?"

"I don't know. She once told me that in front of the children, couples should make it look like they agree on things. She's a psychologist, isn't she? A counselor at a youth consultation center, right?"

"So, where is Grandma going to stay?" I asked.

"I don't know. She said that even without a reservation, she should be able to stay in some hotel or other, and she just left."

"The other day she was telling me that Uncle Sadao's second son Shimpei lives in Fukuoka: wouldn't he put her up?"

"We did talk about that. She said that he has a restaurant, so it would be *yayakoshii* to stay with him and that a hotel would be better."

That's when I remembered that at the *hoji*, I had told Oharu-baasan that there are a lot of yakuza in Fukuoka. Her train of thought must have gone like this: Since Ichiro and Shinpei were on good terms, Ichiro may have gone to Fukuoka. So far, so good. But I don't think that means she has to worry about him joining the yakuza. I don't know that much about Japanese society anymore: Do young people these days take joining the yakuza lightly? The yakuza frighten even me. So what could my eighty-seven-year-old mother do, rushing down there with her cane?

I had no idea what to do. I couldn't understand why I had to get caught up in such a *yayakoshii* matter when I was away from home. Ah—family! I figured that even though Ichiro had run away from home, he was still young and had stamina. That meant that the most serious concern was finding Oharu-baasan, who had gone missing while trying to track down her runaway grandson. I decided that the fastest way to do that would be for me to go look for her. If I found her, the two of us could go to Chizu's house together. I needed to go to galleries in Osaka and Kyoto, so I had to go west anyway. And fortunately, I still had five days before my appointments at the galleries.

"I'll go look for Grandma," I told Nobuko. "I'll go to Fukuoka tomorrow morning."

9

I decided to call my family in Los Angeles to let them know that my schedule in Japan had changed so they wouldn't worry that I had gone missing. I had no idea what hotel I'd be staying at in Fukuoka, but I thought that at least I should let them know that for the next three days I wouldn't be at Chizu's as planned.

My husband David answered the phone.

"Things are a real mess," I blurted out.

"What are you talking about?"

"Ahh . . . it seems that Chizu's son Ichiro gave up on taking college entrance exams and ran away from home before he even graduated from high school. When Grandma heard about it, she got all worked up worrying about him joining the yakuza or something and went off with her cane—I mean, *holding* her cane . . ."

"What do you mean, '*holding* her cane'?"

"Ahh . . . she always . . . even though we bought her a cane . . . she never uses it; she just walks around with it tucked under her arm, so that's why I said that. Anyway, I got a call from Nobuko this morning and she said that Grandma had gone off to Fukuoka in Kyushu."

"Why on earth would she go to Fukuoka? I mean, there's no reason to think that Ichiro ran away to Fukuoka, is there?"

"That's the thing—"

"Or any reason to think that he would join the yakuza, for that matter. Is Grandma planning on getting into a fight with the yakuza? Or is she just going to lecture Ichiro?"

"I don't know."

"Telling a kid like that that so-and-so-chan, the child of Mr. What's-his-name, studied hard and got ahead is not going to do any good. But of course, that's all Grandma would be able to say. Do you know where she is?"

"I'm going to Fukuoka to look for her tomorrow. I was just calling you to let you know that I won't be getting to Chizu's place for a few more days."

David was silent for a while, then suddenly, in a loud voice, he exclaimed, "Hey! I've got a good idea! Let's have John talk to Ichiro. He's a 'double,' so he looks different from everyone in Japan and knows how it feels to stick out. I must say, he never ran away from home in high school, though."

"What do you mean—what about the night he went to stay over at Tony's house and disappeared?"

"Well, that kind of thing doesn't really count."

"Maybe it doesn't count to *you*, but just thinking about it makes me shudder even now. And at the time, you were pretty worked up, too."

"Yeah, I guess you're right. John was rather delinquent. But that's why he might be able to understand the feelings of a troubled teenager and really be able to talk to him. Ichiro might be taking a closer look at society than you think and be tired of all the conformity he sees. If John brought Ichiro to his apartment in Tokyo and they lived together for a week or so, it might open Ichiro's eyes to this whole other world."

"That may be, but I'm sure that high-and-mighty Professor Tatsuo, who never accepts any blame for anything, would tell us not to stick our noses in where they're not wanted. He's always speaking at conferences, flying all over the world like he's trying to win a Nobel prize. He can't be paying much attention to his students, so he must give his family even less. He probably feels that he can't be bothered worrying about his home life. Then, all of a sudden, he finds out that his son is saying he won't go to college. He blows up. Strikes the boy. Since he's a college professor, they can't report it to the police. You know, in Japan, a wife won't call the police just because her husband hits their kids a few times. It wouldn't look respectable. I hear that a lot of college professors abuse their wives and children. And when boys reach puberty, they can be too much for their mother to handle if the father isn't at home. It's no use Tatsuo getting angry now. Remember us with John? You were at home and he was still that much trouble."

"Well, why don't you talk to John about it? I'll call him."

John came to the phone.

"Listen, John. Things are a real mess," I said to him in Japanese.

"What?" came back the response in sleepy English.

"Ahh . . . it's your cousin Ichiro . . . we don't know where he is," I continued on in Kansai-ben. "You see, Grandma Oharu got the idea that he might have gone to Fukuoka so she went there, but we're all just running around in circles. I wonder what on earth Nobuko was really saying." Without realizing it, I had begun talking to myself.

"Mom, I have absolutely no idea what you're trying to say. What's your point? You say Grandma went to Kyushu?" This much had been in Japanese. "*So what?*" Back to Japanese: "So she went to Kyushu."

"You see, Ichiro ran away from home, so she took off, saying that she would catch him and give him a good talking to so that he wouldn't become a member of the yakuza. But at her age, she'll do nothing but get in the way, so now the first thing that has to be done is for me to go look for the one who went looking for the runaway. So I was talking to Daddy just now, and you know, you sometimes were rebellious when you were in high school, and you have experience teaching in a Japanese high school so you know about the way high school students feel, and you recently took pictures of yakuza. So you know how to treat that kind of person, and that's why I want you to come back here quick and try to calm Ichiro down."

"Yakuza? I should think that yakuza make more money than freelance photojournalists like me, don't they? Anyway, there're two ways of joining the yakuza. One way is to drop out of high school and join a gang right away. The other way is to get into a top-level college like Tokyo University or Waseda or Keio, and then after graduating, you become a good government official, and finally, once you've joined the Liberal Democratic Party, you join the yakuza. Waiting until after going to college to join the yakuza is not at all economical, when you consider all the money you have to spend on college tuition, and before that, on cram schools, plus the money you have to hand over to the yakuza; all together, that can come to about five hundred million yen. So as long as you're going to join the yakuza anyway, wouldn't it make more sense just to drop out of high school? You can't be telling Ichiro how to live his life. How old is he now? He must be seventeen or eighteen. He's already a grown-up. I couldn't try to talk him out of anything. It's late here; I'm going to bed. Goodnight, Mom."

And with that, that rascal John hung up on me.

10

If, as Oharu-baasan thought, Ichiro had really joined the yakuza, how did she think she could get him out? She certainly couldn't do that on her own. So the following morning, I stuffed a week's worth of clothing in a bag. Of course, I made sure to pack the slides of my paintings, too.

As I was bustling about getting ready to leave, the phone on the counter rang. How *yayakoshii!*

I picked up the receiver, only to hear a young male voice identifying himself as an officer from the Azabu Police Station, which is in the same trendy area of Tokyo as John's apartment.

My heart skipped a beat. I figured that something had happened to my mother, or that this was about Ichiro. The piece of candy I had in my mouth seemed to stick in my throat.

The voice began interrogating me: "Ahh . . . do you live at number 18, Roppongi 7-chome?"

"Yes, I do."

"And does a person called Jesus Krist live there?"

What the . . . ? "This is not a church, so the Lord Jesus has not honored us with his presence," I answered.

"I'm not talking about the Lord Jesus. I'm inquiring about Mr. Jesus Krist."

"I've never heard of anyone by that name," I replied, and then it occurred to me that it might be the name of one of my son's friends—only the policeman's pronunciation of the name was so completely different that I hadn't recognized it at first. One of John's friends is named Christopher Joseph, and I think he's usually called Chris. Perhaps the policeman had just reversed the order of his first and last name?

"So whose house is that?" he asked politely.

"My son's."

"And your son's name is?"

"John."

"Is your son in?"

"No, he's in America now . . . Did this Jesus person do something?"

"Yes, a traffic violation. Mr. Jesus was involved in a traffic violation."

"What kind?"

I could not afford to get involved with someone else's affairs at a time like this, but I wanted to find out if he had caused an accident.

"Ahh . . . he was running on the sidewalk."

What an anticlimax! Lots of people run on the sidewalk. So I pointed this out.

"Everybody runs on the sidewalk."

"He was on a bike."

"What's wrong with that?"

"It's against the law."

"Huh?"

"And what is your name?"

"Why do you have to know my name?" My voice went up a full octave as I began to question him, as though I thought that by screeching I could drive away someone else's misfortunes that were about to come tumbling down on me.

"I want to write up a report, so I need that information."

"Get real. I have nothing to do with this, so why do I have to tell you my name? You must have a lot of more important things to do. You're a police officer! This is ridiculous! What a waste of time!" I was so offended that I was screaming. Then suddenly, I flashed back to the war and how terrifying the police were then, and I started trembling at the thought that he might threaten me.

After a moment of silence, the policeman said, "You're right," and simply hung up.

I was rather shocked. During the war, if we answered questions with even the slightest smile on our faces, the police would scold us roundly for not being serious. And then if we lashed out at them instead of apologizing, they would hit us.

I hurriedly got dressed, then donned my black beret—the hat that made young blacks in America identify me as a Black Panther. After locking the apartment door, I went down to the street and caught a cab for Tokyo Station. The Yaesu side, to be precise.

This is a really *yayakoshii* place—in all the world, this is the place I end up spending the most time wandering around, even though I speak the language! Coming from the suburbs of Los Angeles, where I go everywhere by car and there is not a living soul on the streets during the day, I'm totally out of my element in this terminal, a tiny little space teeming with people, so it takes me forever to do anything.

With my travel bag in my right hand, I plowed my way through the throngs of travelers who were as lost as I was and finally made it to the place where tickets are sold. There were lines of people at all of the windows. I got into the shortest line. The person behind the window was a young man of about twenty-five. When the elderly man in front of me, who spoke in the Hiroshima dialect, was finished, it was at last my turn.

"Listen; I'd like a round-trip ticket to Fukuoka on the Shinkansen bullet train," I said.

"Ma'am, there's no station called Fukuoka on the Shinkansen line."

"Huh? So how can I get to Fukuoka?"

"It's Hakata. Hakata," said the ticket seller curtly.

Unaware of what I was doing, I stood there slack-jawed, staring at the man's flat little nose. I was astounded that there wasn't a station called Fukuoka, when years ago, in elementary school I had learned that Fukuoka was one of Japan's six largest cities.

"Why doesn't it stop in Fukuoka?"

"People going to Fukuoka get off at Hakata."

"Then what line do they transfer to?"

"Huh?" The ticket seller's nostrils flared and he looked wretched—like he didn't have a clue as to what to do with me. Finally he said, "When you get off the train you're *in* Fukuoka, Ma'am."

"Oh? They really made it *yayakoshii*, didn't they? I wonder why they didn't think to name it Fukuoka? I bet there are a lot of people like me, aren't there?"

Without deigning to answer, he merely asked, "Will that be for one?"

"Yes."

"That will be ¥38,960."

He handed me my two boarding tickets along with the express tickets.

I didn't get a seat reservation. It's easiest just to get on the first train that comes in. I realized that Oharu-baasan has always known that. She told me that she always goes to the food section in the basement of the Daimaru Department store on the Yaesu side of the station and buys a bento boxed lunch there before getting on a train. I, on the other hand, always get a reservation when I'm going to the Kansai area so I never have time to get a bento from a department store because I'm always in a rush to catch my train. That's why I don't like reserved seats: *they* determine the time, not you. But then once I get on the train, I remember that I forgot to buy a bento. I never plan ahead, so I always end up buying the awful bentos they sell on the train.

All the same, I still couldn't get over the fact that up until now, I had never realized that the name of the Shinkansen station in Fukuoka is Hakata. Would someone like that really be able to search out her elderly mother? I started feeling a lot less confident.

Shortly after the train had passed the Izu area, where glimpses of bamboo groves and fields of mandarin orange trees flashed past between the tunnels, Mount Fuji came clearly into view, wearing a cap of snow above the reddish-purple expanse of its base. As always, I was overwhelmed by its majestic figure—far more than I could ever be by any painting, no matter how great the artist. While everyone else in the car slept, I alone stood up and kept my gaze fixed on the mountain until it passed out of sight. I am neither an ultranationalist nor a Japanese person who's lived overseas too long and now thinks of her motherland in terms of "Fujiyama" and "Geisha." But I find the mountain aesthetically terrifying. Even paintings of Fuji by great artists like Umehara Ryuzaburo and Yokoyama Taikan don't quite seem to capture it. It is the one subject I am resigned to not even trying to paint.

After a while, the train reached the area around Shin Fuji Station and Miho no Matsubara, where the scenery was marred by a confusing array of spherical and cylindrical gas tanks, rows of metal poles holding up high-voltage electrical cables, and a forest of chimneys belching smoke. Who said the Japanese revere beauty? The sensibility that allowed the most famous aesthetic symbol of Japan to be maliciously destroyed like this was the same as that which gave permission to put up tall buildings in the ancient capital of Kyoto. Perhaps this was the fault of the Liberal Democrats—the political party that had been in power almost continuously since shortly after World War II. Daishowa Paper Mill, Honshu Paper Manufacturing, Onoda Cement, Esso Oil, Toshiba, something-or-other chemical—what nerve these companies have, shamelessly putting their names on their factories' smokestacks without fear for their reputation! This was just too insensitive! The contrast with the area's natural beauty was just too great. If they're going to do this, I almost wish that Fuji would erupt and sweep this hideous scene totally off the map, I thought.

Seeing the name Tagonoura used in the name of a warehouse and painted brazenly on the side of the building was enough to make me weep. For the view of Mount Fuji from Tagonoura was made famous by the earliest collection of Japanese poetry, the *Manyoshu*, in a poem by the great eighth century poet Yamabe-no-sukune Akahito:

When one looks up into the expanse of the heavens
At the peak of Mount Fuji in Suruga
Which has stood majestic, lofty and exalted
Ever since the heavens and earth were parted
The passing sun is hidden
Nor can the light of the moon be seen

Even the white clouds hesitate to approach
Yet the snows fall incessantly

Let us recount the story of Fuji's peak
Handing down the tale
From generation to generation

Coda
Coming out from Tagonoura Bay
I see snow falling
Pure and white
On Fuji's lofty peak

One of the most famous Japanese folk tales, a story about a heavenly maiden whose robe of feathers was stolen while she was bathing, was also set in the area near Mount Fuji. Given the view I was looking at from the train, I wondered what we could possibly say to children in the future when we try to teach them the traditional culture to be handed down "from generation to generation" in the form of such poems and folktales.

These companies polluted everything in this area and turned the sea into sludge, and then the president of one of them was able to take the money he'd made doing this and buy Van Gogh's *Sunflowers*. I just about fell over when I heard that. I have to question that company president's aesthetic sense. Rather, I should say I don't think he *has* a sense of beauty. He probably would have been happy with anything that had the name Van Gogh on it. It was probably nothing more than an investment to him.

11

By the time I reached Hakata, the sun had already set. I went down the stairs in the station and out the Chikushi Exit. I was quite surprised to see a virtual forest of skyscrapers before my eyes, with neon signs flickering atop and down the side of nearly every building. Traffic was also quite heavy, and I suddenly was petrified by the thought that this, too, was a very large city. I was all alone, in the dark, with no idea of which way was east or west—extremely insecure; my legs trembled, and I began to worry that I just might dissolve like a slug that's been sprinkled with salt. I realized that walking around in this den of thieves (at least that's what it looked like to me), looking for Oharu-baasan, would be no easy task. Even if I hailed a taxi, I would not know where to tell it to go. I decided that the first thing I would have to do is to call each of the hotels in Fukuoka and ask if she was staying there tonight.

But before doing that, I needed to make my own arrangements for a place to stay for the night. Among the many tall buildings surrounding me, a couple had neon signs identifying them as hotels, so I decided to go to the nearest one, the K Hotel. Not having a reservation, I was relieved to find that they had a vacancy.

It was not yet dinner time, so I figured I'd put my luggage in my room and then start calling all the hotels in Fukuoka, but first I thought I'd take a walk and check out the hotels nearby. As I was walking toward the reception desk in the lobby, I spied a short old woman with a protruding belly and trousers that looked like old-fashioned *momohiki* pants with a drawstring at the waist; she was almost clinging to one corner of the counter as she talked to the woman handling reception. It had to be my mother.

As soon as I saw her, I cried to myself, 'Oh, how lucky! Lucky! To have found her so quickly!' Out loud, I shouted "Obaachan!" in a very excited voice.

She turned in the direction of my voice with a suspicious look on her face. She has cataracts, so apparently she couldn't make out that it was me right away. Just as I'd guessed, she, too, was staying in the hotel closest to the station.

"It's me. Me-gu-mi."

"Why are you . . . in a place like this? Do you have some business here?"

She had a puzzled look on her face, but showed not the slightest trace of fatigue. How lucky to have that kind of a disposition, I thought with envy. On my part, I was so mentally and physically exhausted that my legs were trembling.

"No. Nobuko phoned me and said that you had gone to Fukuoka looking for Ichiro, so I came to look for you. Ichiro is a boy and he's young, so he's got plenty of stamina, but you don't, Obaachan."

'Why do I have to explain all of this to you?' I thought; 'Shouldn't you be the one doing the explaining?' Taking my mother's arm, I pulled her over to the sofa in the middle of the lobby and sat down.

"What were you asking the woman at reception?"

"Huh? I was asking her where the yakuza headquarters are in this city."

"How could you ask something like that?"

"That's the thing. That woman at the front desk didn't give me an answer."

"She probably thought you were a little touched in the head, you know. If you had found out, were you planning on going there?"

"Sure. I thought it would be all right to go and talk a little."

"Obaachan, you're letting your imagination run away with you. Why does Ichiro have to join the Fukuoka yakuza? Why Fukuoka? You've really caused a lot of trouble! On top of that, you didn't say what hotel you'd be staying at, so of course, everyone was upset. So, since I was planning on going west to Kansai, I decided to go look for you while I was at it. But why Fukuoka?"

"Huh? Well, you see, yesterday evening I called Shimpei and asked if Ichiro was there, and he said he wasn't. It seems Chizu had called him, too. Then he told me to come over for dinner, so I went. Of course, their apprentice or whatever picked me up and brought me back here by car. The restaurant is called Pistol and it served French food."

"What? Pistol? That's a very scary name, isn't it? . . . Isn't . . . isn't it Bistro?"

"That's it. That's it. But who cares about stuff like that? I asked Shimpei if he had any idea of where else Ichiro might go, but he said he didn't know. Where would he have gone? Honestly!"

"Well then, let's get ourselves some dinner. Then we can call Chizu and ask her to let us stay at her place tomorrow."

"You know, Tatsuo will probably be at home with a sour look on his face, and his mother is there, too, so it won't be very comfortable. It might be better to go back to Tokyo as soon as we can."

"Why, we don't need to be *that* reserved with them, do we? His mother is quite old and can't hear very well, so we don't need to worry about imposing. I stay there a lot. I suppose with this kind of thing, that Tatsuo is sure to be really upset, but the house was built before the war, so it's really big . . . Wouldn't it be better for Chizu if you were there for her? Now, for dinner, you'd prefer *nihon-shoku*, wouldn't you?" I said, using direct translations of the words Japanese and food.

"What do you mean by *nihon-shoku*? It's called *washoku*, you know."

"Right. In America, we talk about French and Chinese food, so the direct translation just popped out."

"We could go to Shimpei's place again."

"I don't believe it! Just the other day you were going on and on about the cholesterol in French cookies! How could you ask for French food? You had it just yesterday, didn't you?"

"It was really good. He held off on the butter for me. I bet it's expensive." She blinked her eyes repeatedly and stared off into space.

"If we go there, we'd have to take a taxi and buy something to give them. That's too *yayakoshii*. For starters, we'd have to talk about Uncle Sadao. Also, I've never met Shimpei. I couldn't stand that. So let's just have *washoku*."

I could not stand the thought of getting involved in any more of my relatives' affairs.

12

The two of us got on the Shinkansen at Hakata. The whole time we were on the train, Oharu-baasan talked my ear off, repeating—for the third time since I had arrived back in Japan—her stories about the missionary from long ago, her complaints about her dentist and her description of the people in her retirement home. After arriving at Shin-Kobe Station, we switched to the Hankyu line, and from Shukugawa Station we took a taxi, so it was almost evening before we reached Chizu's house.

Of course I was also concerned about Ichiro, but since I'd found my mother, I felt like my real goal had been achieved, and, thinking that I simply must not let her go again, I made sure that I got her safely to Chizu's home in Shukugawa, a scenic area with lots of flowering cherry trees and pines.

Chizu's house was surrounded by a granite wall on which a Chinese juniper hedge had been planted; in the middle of this fence there was an old cypress gate with a small wooden door at its side. No sooner had I pressed the doorbell on it than Chizu came out—as if she had been waiting for us.

As soon as she saw Chizu's face, Oharu-baasan gave her a formulaic greeting: "The two of us will be imposing upon you. Much obliged."

"What? It is you two! I thought I heard a taxi, " said Chizu bluntly in a tired-sounding voice. Her oval-shaped face looked very much like our father's.

"We came in one, but it's already gone. Why?" I asked.

"Oh? Tatsuo is going to Tokyo by plane from Itami Airport today, and then the day after tomorrow he's flying to Paris for a conference, so I just called a cab for him."

"What? If I'd known, I'd have had it wait. But in any case, this is a fine mess, isn't it? I'm surprised you agreed to let Tatsuo go." Even though I had imagined Tatsuo doing this sort of thing, I was quite surprised when he actually went.

Then, in an attempt to start over, I said, "Well, it's been a while. You okay?" As I spoke, I took a good look at my younger sister's face. She was pale and looked tired. She had more wrinkles around the edges of her large eyes. She probably hadn't been sleeping properly.

"Yeah, well."

"You haven't heard anything from Ichiro?"

"No. I'm really worried. Where could he be? What's he thinking? They're a fine pair," she said, gazing toward entrance, where Tatsuo was waiting.

Since no one was paying her any attention, Oharu-baasan had gone ahead of us into the house, and we could hear her greeting Tatsuo in a high-pitched voice that sounded rather tense.

I followed her, walking with Chizu along the flagstone path—which was flanked by an attractive array of boxwood, azaleas and ornamental bamboo—to the entranceway of the house, where Tatsuo was sitting on the step up from the entrance. After greeting him, I said, "This is a fine mess, isn't it? Do you have to go to Paris?" From my point of view, his taking off like this seemed so strange that I cut right to the point.

"Yeah; I was asked to present my research at this conference a year ago, so I can't refuse now," Tatsuo answered—without showing the least sign that he was perturbed by his son's disappearance. He probably hadn't told his colleagues that his son had run away.

"I'm so glad that the two of you have come," said Chizu.

I, too, breathed a sigh of relief. Although I'd said things indicating that I put some of the blame for this situation on Tatsuo, I was glad he was leaving, since then neither my mother nor I would have to deal with this difficult person while we were here. Chizu's mother-in-law was eighty-eight years old and in far worse shape than Oharu-baasan, so she wouldn't be much of a problem, either, and we could feel totally at ease during our stay.

I wasn't all that worried about Ichiro. I felt that it wouldn't be such a big deal to scour the country for him. Japan is only about the size of California and has four times as many people, so if we just went out looking, following the old Japanese adage that "The dog who trots about is sure to find a bone," we'd be able to find him, I thought.

Then I was struck by another possibility: what if he went overseas? I decided to check with the two of them. "Listen, Ichiro doesn't have a passport, does he?"

"No, he doesn't. He never had the chance to go abroad. What with going to cram schools and all, he never had the time," my younger sister said pensively, her hands pulled back into the sleeves of her loosely woven lavender wool cardigan, as she'd become a bit chilled standing in the entranceway to the house.

The bell next to the gate rang.

Chizu ran out, and when she opened the wooden door, a taxi driver who looked about thirty-five greeted us loudly.

Chizu turned back and yelled, "Tatsuo, the taxi is here."

I tried to reassure Tatsuo. "If anything happens, Chizu will let you know. I'll be imposing upon your hospitality for the next week, so I'll be here when Chizu needs someone to talk things over with. Does she know the number of your hotel in Paris?"

"Yeah, she knows," said Tatsuo, his thin, handsome face tense under his rimless glasses. Then he strode off, a small traveling bag in his right hand, another bag slung over his left shoulder. I was once again struck by how tall he was. I realized that this was why Ichiro is so tall.

At last we were able to relax as we settled in the living room, where Chizu made us some *hojicha* roasted tea.

From the hall next to the living room I heard a swishing sound. About five seconds later, I heard it again. I was thinking that perhaps someone was spraying something with an atomizer when suddenly Chizu's mother-in-law appeared at the threshold of the living room. Her hair, which was still half black, was cut short like a man's. She was wearing a baggy beige wool skirt. She looked like she had been quite a beauty when she was young. She had a thin face with a nice, tall nose. Tatsuo looked like her, and Ichiro's face was like hers, too.

Both my mother and I greeted her, saying "It's been such a long time," but she just kept standing there with a blank expression on her face.

In a loud voice that sounded like she was giving someone a good scolding, Chizu yelled, "Mother, this is my mother and older sister." It was enough to startle us.

Then Chizu turned to us and said, "Her hearing keeps getting worse, so you have to talk loudly or she won't be able to hear you. And these days, her memory is fading pretty badly, so she doesn't clearly remember who people are."

"Does that mean you haven't told her about Ichiro?"

"No, I haven't. That would only make things even more

yayakoshii."

When their daughter Mika—a first-year high school student who had grown quite tall since I'd last seen her—came home from school, we had supper.

Once again Oharu-baasan began complaining about how hard a time she had because her dentures didn't fit right. What she really meant was that she wanted to take them out. By this time, I was completely fed up with this particular grievance of hers, so I put into action a plan I'd come up with.

"Obaachan, there's no need to stand on ceremony here, so why don't you just borrow a small dish and ask if they don't mind if you take them out," I suggested.

"Oh, a small dish? Mika, will you bring her one." At this prompt by Chizu, Mika quickly put her slender body into motion, sending her shoulder-length black hair swishing around as she went to the kitchen to bring back a small dish. Oharu-baasan then removed her dentures, put them in the dish and placed them on one end of the cupboard behind her.

After dinner, Oharu-baasan turned to Chizu's mother-in-law and said, "*Hu hushed he honhee hish hahuo hon.*"

'You had to go talk! Great!' I thought. Since Chizu had told her to talk in a loud voice, my mother was spewing out more air than usual as she spoke, and that made it even harder to understand what she was saying. All the same, I got the general drift, so I translated for her in a loud voice.

"My mother says that you must be lonely with Tatsuo gone."

"What?"

So I had to yell it again. As this process was repeated, we all became hoarse and I kept asking for tea, and then the old ladies would see me drinking and they'd drink more tea, too.

13

Oharu-baasan said that she was especially tired today so she was going to go to bed before me, and after the two old women had gone upstairs, the conversation turned to our primary concern—Ichiro. I didn't understand the situation in Japan very well, so I asked Chizu about it.

"Chii-chan," I said, using her pet name, "this is your specialty, so I don't think I should meddle, but . . . do lots of kids run away from home these days?"

"Well, there are some. These days, everyone's got money, so I guess it's on the increase."

"If a kid like that comes to you, how do you counsel them?"

"The kids don't normally come by themselves . . . If they've run away from home, they never come by themselves. In very rare cases, the parents notice the problem before the kid actually runs away and bring the kid in. It all depends on the parents. Even though I'm a counselor, Tatsuo could care less—about the family anyway. Also, it's really hard because if something he doesn't like happens, he explodes. He's so difficult," Chizu explained, her bony shoulders drooping as she let out a sigh.

Difficult is just another way of saying inflexible, haughty

and ostentatious—all rolled into one.

"Oneichan," Chizu said, calling me the affectionate term for an older sister, "I quit my job as a counselor three months ago. You see, Tatsuo's mother is getting harder to handle."

Right then, I suddenly remembered something that happened during the summer vacation just before John entered high school: he went missing one night. It had been a long time ago—more than ten years earlier, but I still shudder just recalling it. That day, he was supposed to stay over at his friend Tony's house as he often did. At around midnight, just as we were falling asleep, the phone rang. It was Tony's mother, calling to say that John was not in Tony's room. Tony said that John had arranged to meet some friends in the park and had invited Tony to join them, but he hadn't gone along with John. Hours had passed since then and John had not come back, so Tony told his parents what had happened when they got home from a party. What an uproar ensued! Starting at midnight, we called around to the parents of every single friend we could think of to check, but no one knew where John was. Even though we had disturbed these people, they kindly started calling around for us, too.

That night, my husband David went searching in parks and on the beach, looking in deep ditches and driving up into the mountains, thinking that John might have been kidnapped. At the time, there was someone on the loose who'd taken a number of young people away in a car and killed them—what Americans call a serial killer. We were worried sick that John had been caught by him.

We have a second child who is autistic, so we couldn't split up and both search for John. As I waited at home, impatience became intertwined with despair, frazzling my nerves. Feeling

I had no other recourse, I finally called the police. The officer who answered told me that they would not begin a search for someone until they had been missing for twenty-four hours or more.

Now twenty-four hours is a very long time. I don't suppose anyone would drive a car for twenty-four hours straight, but if they did, they could go from here to Mexico, or up to Oregon or Washington, as well as down to New Mexico, Texas, Arizona, or Utah. When I thought about it that way, I realized that the police could not be counted on for anything, and my blood ran cold. I then called the emergency room at two nearby hospitals. There was no one there who fit John's description.

My mind raced. Our other son was brain-damaged. If we lost the son who was normal, where should we go from there? Beset by such thoughts, I hit the depths of despair. I wondered why I had gone through labor twice when I felt I had given birth to nothing but scum.

I began to think about his motives. I had never told John what he should become in the future—if he had just led a normal life like a normal human being, I would have been satisfied. I have my own life, too. I don't plan on devoting my entire life to caring for my autistic son, so I wouldn't ask John to take care of his younger brother either. If I made him do that, there is no way he could have his own life's dream. All the same, his brother is of the same flesh and blood, so I figured that he must feel psychologically burdened. Still, I was sure that both David and I had clearly told John we had no particular expectations of him in that way.

Had he really gone missing of his own free will or had he been kidnapped? I had no idea.

I think it was about five o'clock in the morning—when we were completely exhausted and at our wits' end—that the telephone finally rang. As David picked up the receiver, he told me that if it was the police, we needed to brace ourselves for the news that they had found John's dead body. But when he answered, he started waving his right hand back and forth, signaling me that this was not the case. Then he said, "Yes, Mrs. Whitfield. Is that so? Then I'll try calling there."

Mrs. Whitfield was the mother of another friend of John's. She had kindly called to let us know that her son had just remembered that he had last seen John with a boy called Max, who lived in a house near the downtown area. Apparently, she hadn't slept a wink since we'd woken her up with our call.

We had already woken up so many people that we didn't feel we should disturb anyone else this early in the morning, so we waited until seven before calling Max's house and learning from Max's father, who had been totally unaware of our panic, that John was all right. Then, starting with the family at whose home John was supposed to be staying, we called all the other parents whom we'd checked with to reassure them that John was all right. It turned out that John had been playing hide-and-seek with some kids—actually big kids—who lived near the downtown area, and it got so late that John couldn't go back to Tony's, so he ended up spending the night at Max's house. He thought that it didn't make any difference where he stayed, since Tony's parents were at a party and would be getting home late; he figured they wouldn't notice that he wasn't there and wouldn't worry.

David took the car over and brought John back, but when he got home and I hugged him, John made a strange face, as if to say he didn't know what all the fuss was about. I guess this is what is meant by the proverb, "A child cannot understand a parent's love."

It was because of that experience that I asked Chizu, "Did you put in a request for a police search?"

"No. We couldn't do something that embarrassing, could we? Tatsuo has his reputation to protect. It would be a fine mess if it got into the papers. And it would affect Ichiro's future, too; if he was the subject of a police investigation, it could cause problems for him later on."

She was my own sister and yet she didn't have any idea of what was important—I was quite disappointed. Was she thinking that his life was not in danger because Japan is a safe country? What kind of a counselor was she? I began worrying whether she was actually qualified to be a counselor. Was this a result of Tatsuo's influence?

She also had no idea how lucky she was that her child was normal. She wasn't grateful for her good fortune in having a child who could stand on his own, walk, put on his own clothes and communicate his intentions. The moment Ichiro had communicated his intentions, his father hit him on the head. Because his counselor mother wouldn't protect him. It's no wonder that it seems to him that all of society is against him. That's the way youth is. Because they don't know the world, they are very insecure; that is, they have no confidence in themselves.

"You two—you don't have any idea how lucky you are to have a normal child. You're not even grateful for that. You don't know how much we thought, 'if only Ken could talk,' or 'if only he could go to school by himself.' Japanese people who move to Los Angeles often proudly go around telling people that their children were first graders in Japan but were put into second grade in America, but I always felt that it was a little strange and wondered what they were bragging about. Our Ken is nowhere near normal grade level, yet we never thought that kind of thing. In special ed, there are kids of all different ages in a single class."

"Yes, but Japanese society isn't like that. People can't accept it if everyone else isn't exactly the same. Oneichan, you just don't know. You left Japan thirty years ago. You're like Rip Van Winkle. Of course there are vocational schools for people who want to become construction workers or photographers, but the parents who send their kids there are, well, *different*. So normal parents don't feel comfortable unless their children go to college. Once the kids graduate, they can go in whatever direction they like and become farmers or carpenters or whatever else they wanted to do from the beginning. College is for the parents. Especially when they're teaching at a college like Tatsuo. They've got colleagues," said Chizu. To me, it sounded like utter nonsense.

"If you've got a child like Ken, there's no way you can keep up appearances like that. In the institution Ken was in before, they admitted a boy who was a little bit smarter than the rest. Then out of the blue, one of the people who worked there said that he'd seen the new boy raping another patient. Of course, the state government agency in charge of the institution came and investigated, but not a single patient in that room could talk. Anyway, instead of worrying about who did what to whom, what they were most afraid of was AIDS. Everyone kicked up a fuss and said that he should be tested, so they did a blood test on the rapist. But then when we said we wanted to be told the results, the agency insisted that they had to strictly protect the rapist's privacy, so they wouldn't tell us. It was only when we pushed them, asking if they were going to ignore the rights of the victim, that they told us that they had not detected the AIDS virus in the rapist's blood.

"Then all of a sudden, the state government ordered the institution closed, and they told us that we had to pick Ken up within twenty-four hours. There was no way we could bring such a violent child back home, so we didn't have a clue as to what we should do and couldn't sleep at all that night. Luckily, the state government agency in charge of the institution found us another place. If that child had come back home, it would have destroyed our family. David's got his heart problems, and we're both pretty old already. If one of us broke a bone, it would be all over. If we—Ken's only advocates—died, that would be the end.

"They say that once a child like that leaves his family, there's a ninety percent chance that he'll suffer some kind of sexual abuse—including rape—at an institution. For girls, the risk might even be higher. One time, Ken had his testicles kicked really hard by one of the workers and his eyes got all bloodshot. We asked who had done it, but the African-American woman director told us it was another patient—even though none of the other patients looked like they could possibly aim a kick at someone's balls. That was clear. The director almost had a nervous breakdown. She seemed to have a pretty good idea of who had done it but she couldn't tell anyone—she couldn't accuse him just on the basis of her intuition. In the end, she changed that man's post. Put him in a room where only one of the six patients couldn't talk. Three months later, they caught someone in the act of molesting the patient who couldn't talk; it was that same worker. Of course, he was put in prison.

"In general, hospitals and institutions don't check the references of the people they hire, and of course, America is a very big country. It's really hard to check on people who've come from out of state. Some people even have a friend pose as a former employer and ask him to speak highly of them. I suppose you don't have to worry about things like that if you live in Japan."

Chizu looked shocked and, gazing steadily at my face, said, "Oneichan, you've been through a lot. I had no idea things were that bad for you. I could never be a social worker or a counselor in a place like that. I guess compared to that, our situation seems like heaven, doesn't it?"

"Well, everyone in your family is healthy, and you have normal people as well as your children to talk things over with. Once you enter the world of the handicapped—well, I suppose there are differences in degree within Japan—but there are all sorts of problems. I guess it's not as bad as in America, though. By now, my hide has gotten tough and nothing shocks me anymore.

"I suppose you'll have a hard time with Ichiro from now on, but it won't really count; that mother-in-law of yours will be more trouble. You have to be ready to go through the same kind of thing with her that we had to go through with Ken. But then again, she's old and doesn't have that much longer to live. Ken is much younger than we are. John knows that and sometimes it bothers him."

I could hear the wind rustling the branches of the pine and maple trees in the garden, while the cries of a swarm of crickets chirping reverberated in my ears. I couldn't hear insects singing like this in the apartment in Tokyo. I fondly recalled autumn nights of long ago in Japan. Even though I was in someone else's house and we had become somewhat estranged from each other, I think I felt a tinge of nostalgia because my younger sister and my mother were under the same roof with me.

"Life is short, so if you don't let Ichiro do what he wants, you'll regret it later. I think that if he's sent to a famous college just so his parents can show off and is not allowed to do what he wants, he'll be unhappy the rest of his life. It's all right for a kid to do what his parents say and stay in college or get a job at a big company if the kid himself is satisfied with that. But Ichiro is not content to do that and is saying that he doesn't want to take any college entrance exams, right? You shouldn't make him, but then you need to tell him that if he makes his own decision about what to do, he has to take responsibility for it. Anyway, I wonder where he is? He's been missing for four days now, hasn't he? You really should put in a request for a police search."

In America, none of the people around me are from what would be called normal families in Japan, so when I come back to this country, people always ask me what my husband does, and when I tell them that he's a writer, they ask if he's working at a company—it really floors me how few regular Japanese understand anything about working independently. That's why I thought I might be a good person to help out in Ichiro's case and had been giving Chizu advice.

Chizu listened in silence, but inwardly, she seemed to be in turmoil. The dream she'd had for her son had been shattered, and there didn't seem to be anything she could do to change that.

"Well, I'm still going to wait a little longer."

Really! What kind of counseling had Chizu been doing? Had she just been advising all the children she saw to adapt to this twisted society?

I decided to change the subject.

"About Obaachan—I was talking to her when she came to visit me the other day. We were talking about Auntie Ikuyo's *hoji* anniversary ceremony, and from there, we got to talking about how big and extravagant Auntie's funeral had been, and how silly that was. She said Buddhists were really picky about such things, and that was just the chance I'd been waiting for, so I said, 'Obaachan, you're a Christian, right, so what do you think about having a Christian funeral?' I told her it would be 'parental piety' on her part to decide this now and make things easier for her children to handle when the time came. She told me she hasn't been going to church, so she couldn't do that. Then I told her that I have some friends who are Christians and that I could get them to look for a church near her and suggested that she could start going there regularly on Sundays. Then she started going on and on about denominations, but at this point, I don't think that makes any difference, do you?"

"Just having that conversation was an achievement of sorts."

I'd expected more praise from her than that, but Chizu's thoughts were elsewhere.

14

Whenever I'm staying in a different place, I always find it hard to sleep, but that night, having drunk cup after cup of tea after dinner without giving it a thought, I felt the urge to urinate, and, unable to sleep, kept turning my pillow over. Suddenly I heard Oharu-baasan, who was sleeping next to me, squirming around as if she were getting up.

Then, in a loud, murky voice, she said,

"*Hare on hurse is hiss?*"

"Shh," I said. Then, lowering my voice, I continued: "Listen, you can't go talking in a loud voice in the middle of the night. This is Chizu's house."

"Where is the *hoilet?*"

"Go out into that hallway there; it's in the corner on the right. Be careful." Before I'd finished saying this, however, I heard a thud as she hit the *shoji*. Then there was a rattling as she opened the sliding paper doors. She didn't close them behind her, so the cold mid-November night air came into the room. I pulled the quilt up over my head.

When my mother finally returned, she said, "I almost bumped into the cage sitting there in the hallway."

"Hmmn," I said from the futon. Since I was doing my best

to get to sleep, it wasn't much of a response. Then, thinking that this might be a good time to go to the bathroom, I got up and went. "I shouldn't have had so much tea," I kept telling myself, ruing my carelessness. When I finally made my way back to my futon and was trying to get back to sleep, the fusuma of the room across the hallway began to rattle. It sounded like Chizu's mother-in-law was trying to get out of her room. This being an old house, the shoji and fusuma doors didn't slide smoothly.

Next I heard the swishing sound of her walking. It seemed that she, too, was on her way to the toilet. She'd also had a lot of tea.

Just when I thought things had finally settled down, I heard a strange combination of noises from over where Oharu-baasan was sleeping: "Kghh, ghh, ghh . . . ooh oohn, heeee, munph, munph . . ." I couldn't tell if she was snoring or talking in her sleep, but there certainly was quite a variety of sounds coming out of her.

"Shh," I said. The sounds stopped for a moment but they started up again right away. Figuring there was nothing more I could do, I pulled my futon as far away from hers as I could and moved my pillow to the other end to put as much distance as possible between my head and hers.

About an hour later I again heard the fusuma rattling and a swishing sound from out in the hallway.

When at last a hush had fallen over the house again, my mother, who had been producing an amazingly diverse range of sounds, again wriggled her way out of her futon and then rattled the shoji open. Damn that tea!

As I was wondering if I'd be awake all night, the two old ladies finally both fell into a deep sleep. In better spirits, I, too, finally drifted off just before dawn.

"Hah . . . Hah . . . The evil mother-in-law of Oka, Hanako-san

. . . Nakama, Mitsuhashi, pop-eye Matsuki . . . In-bara-punc . . . a-ll the rage." Suddenly, a loud voice that sounded like a broken microphone reverberated down the hallway. I jumped up out of my futon. In a strange cadence that sounded like a drunk singing the good old Osaka Ondo folk dance song, the raspy, jesting voice was belting out utter nonsense. Three times it repeated the song. Now I was wide-awake. The voice was coming from the vicinity of Ichiro's room, which was near the toilet.

"*Whaa in za hurl? Hrom ho early in za morning? Hinging ho bad*," mumbled Oharu-baasan in a very lethargic, sleepy voice.

"Really! Good grief! How insulting! Who *is* that? Was someone else staying here? And I had just finally gotten to sleep when that fucking idiot starts up. What does he think he's doing at this hour?"

"What? 'Fucking idiot'? I'm sure I taught you not to talk like that!"

"I'm fifty-eight. It's too late to talk to me about my language now. I can say whatever I want when I get mad," I asserted. Then, switching to English, I added, "Oh, shit!"

Apparently, Oharu-baasan didn't understand that.

A bit of light seeped into the room from between the slats in the storm shutters. I turned on the reading lamp near the head—actually, the foot—of my futon and looked at my watch; it was only six thirty. Had a thief or a drunk, knowing that there were only women at home tonight, broken in without our realizing it?

Chizu's mother-in-law was apparently unaware of the situation. 'Being unable to hear isn't all bad,' I thought.

Feeling that we were enveloped in a mystery, my mother and I became rather frightened and debated about what to do in loud whispers. It would be terrible if the singer came into our room, but neither of us was brave enough to go out and look, so maybe it was best to just crawl back into our futons.

After a while, the voice said, "I'm sta-rving; I'm sta-rving; I'm sta-rving." Then, what did he say but, "O-ha-ru-baachan's running around in ci-rcles. O-ha-ru-baachan's running around in ci-rcles."

"*Huh? Wha's hat? He's halking ahoud me, izind he,*" cried my mother as she tossed off her quilt and sat up in her futon, a puzzled look on her face. I couldn't sleep now. This must be something that Ichiro had said into a tape recorder. But who had turned it on? The lad couldn't have just been out drinking, come home drunk, slipped quietly into the house and now be in his own room, could he? Hoping that was the case, I plucked up the courage to go out into the hallway.

When I turned on the hall light, I saw a birdcage in the hallway in front of Ichiro's room; inside it, a large blue bird was making a tapping noise as it pecked at the metal frame of the cage with its sturdy beak.

The bird heard my footsteps, and when I turned on the light, he looked at me and his head began bobbing up and down while he screeched bloody murder. Then he cried, "Thie-f! Thie-f!"

The owner of the mysterious voice was none other than this parrot. I'd never dreamed that the family had this kind of pet. But then again, when Oharu-baasan went to the bathroom, she did say that she'd almost bumped into something like a cage. My dream of Ichiro returning home flew out the window. But who on earth had taught the bird such foolishness?

15

It was now seven o'clock, so we went downstairs. Chizu was up and the aroma of coffee and smoke from grilled fish filled the dining room. Even though this was an old house, the kitchen and dining room had been modernized. The dining room was located between the kitchen and the living room and looked like what we'd call a breakfast room in America.

"Good morning. Boy, that coffee smells good," I exclaimed.

"Good morning. Yeah, Obaachan likes coffee. Did you have a good sleep?" asked Chizu.

"Are you kidding? That parrot woke both of us up so early this morning! It really took us by surprise. I don't know what song he was singing, but we thought it was a drunk. The tune sounded like the Osaka Ondo folk dance song." My eyes were clouded over due to lack of sleep, so I was opening and shutting them as I spoke.

"Oh, yeah! Sorry about that. I forgot about him. No one ever sleeps in that room, and Ichiro gets up at six, so it's not normally a problem. That parrot starts to sing as soon as it starts getting light outside, so if we put him downstairs, we couldn't sleep at all. Especially on weekends. Since Tatsuo's mother can't hear anything anyway, we put him up there."

"When did you get him? You didn't have him last year, did you?"

"No, we didn't. There was a Yuhigaoka High School reunion last November. For the Osaka and Kobe area. One of the alumni I met was a very old lady—she must be about seventy-five—who went to Yuhigaoka before the war when it was a girls' school. She lives in this neighborhood so I know her really well. Anyway, she said she was all alone now and had decided to sell her house and move into a retirement home. Since pets aren't allowed there, she couldn't take her parrot along, so she said she'd give it to me and she did."

"Who taught it that song?"

"That lady, I suppose. It must have been around the time she went to Yuhigaoka, so I guess it would have been about 1935. That would be about when the Osaka Ondo was written. The parrot's song is probably making fun of the Yuhigaoka teachers of that time. She told me that 'the evil mother-in-law of Oka, Hanako-san' was a really strict dance teacher who was always hitting everyone."

I suddenly remembered a terrifying dance teacher who wore her hair up in a bun. "Oh—she was still there when I went to school; she was there! What a scary teacher! She wouldn't have had to do that to teach dance. If she'd made it more fun, we would have all liked dancing. She was straight as an arrow and her name was Oshige Hanako. And, well, 'pop-eye Matsuki' is easy to figure out—that must be the teacher with the bulging eyes. I didn't know her, though. But what does 'In-bara-punc' mean?"

"I couldn't figure it out, either, so I asked that old alumna. 'In' is the English word 'in,' 'bara' is Japanese for 'stomach,' and 'punc' is for 'puncture,' like in a tire that blows out. It means that what's in the stomach's gotten so big it's ready to explode."

Just around the time we were finishing this conversation, Oharu-baasan came into the dining room and mumbled,

"What does it mean to be 'ready to *ekshode*'"? Without her dentures, Oharu-baasan lost some of her consonants.

"Nearing the end of her pregnancy," Chizu and I declared in unison.

"I can't believe they made up that song," said Chizu. "Those kids were ahead of us in that school, so we're supposed to respect them, but even so, I was disgusted when I heard it. And it seems we can't erase it from the parrot's memory. Not now that it's been input. I guess in that way, computers are better—you can delete things from them."

Then Oharu-baasan burst in again with her mumbling. "*Haa—hohee smells good. But, hat 'Oharu-baachan's runnin' around in cir-cles--wha's hat?*"

Chizu and I looked at each other and snickered.

"That—Ichiro must have taught . . . him." Just saying her son's name was enough to move Chizu to tears, so she was half laughing and half crying.

Trying to redirect the conversation, I commented,

"He did quite a job, didn't he. Teaching him to say, 'I'm starving' and 'thief.' Why, that parrot could almost serve as a watchdog, though not where he is now. You should put him downstairs somewhere that's not so secure—where a thief could easily get in. That said, it's a really crude bird, isn't it?"

"*Homma ni,*" Chizu agreed. "Still, I bet parrots like that are really expensive. She told me it came from Central America. Sometimes when he's in the mood, he starts telling a fairy tale: 'Once upon a time, there was an old man and an old woman.' Some of the things he says are pretty long. He only does that on very rare occasions, though. The first time I heard him, I was amazed."

"Oh, I wish Ken had as much of a brain as that parrot," I

quipped, and then suddenly felt sad about being jealous of a bird.

"I thought that maybe it was Ichiro-chan who had come home drunk and, either to surprise us or out of despair, was singing," I added weakly.

"*Hichiro hasn't honhakhed hou het?*" asked Mother, who was still standing.

"No, not a word."

"Did you call his friends?" I asked.

"No. That would be embarrassing, wouldn't it."

"Yes, but if Ichiro-chan suddenly disappeared, wouldn't his friends and teachers think it strange?"

"No. We told the school that he's sick."

Even though she's my sister, I just shook my head. All this covering up must be exhausting, and it also means they can't look for him either.

Then, seemingly out of left field, Oharu-baasan mumbled, "*Hohay, Him hoing home.*"

"Why? You just got here," said Chizu as she poured coffee into Mother's cup.

"It's just possible that Ichiro will call my place." Oharu-baasan mumbled that, too, but if I recorded what she actually said, no one would understand it, so I'll just write it like it was normal speech.

"Really?" said Chizu weakly, her head hanging down.

Oharu-baasan was starting to sit down at the table when she suddenly cried, "Hey! My dentures are gone! I put them right here in a small dish—where did they go?"

"Huh?" Chizu stared at Mother's face with a puzzled expression. "Last night just before I went to bed I found a small dish with nothing in it, so I washed it. Your dentures weren't in it."

Chizu and I looked under the table and chairs and even in the wastebasket in the corner of the room but didn't find them.

When we had given up and the three of us were seated at the table and ready to eat breakfast, we heard the by now familiar swishing sound of feet sliding along the hallway. Chizu's mother-in-law appeared at the entrance of the dining room wearing a long baggy skirt. It seemed that she has Japanese food in the morning; Chizu began putting miso soup and grilled fish on a tray just for her.

Seeing this, the old woman said in a hoarse voice, "Chizu-san, I'm not going to have breakfast this morning."

"Why, Mother?" asked Chizu in a loud voice that sounded like she was scolding. "You don't have an appetite?"

"No, that's not it. Somehow, the inside of my mouth hurts."

"Got a canker sore or something?"

"No, it's my gums."

"Are they swollen?"

"No, they've shrunk."

That was when I figured it out. "Listen—I bet her dentures don't fit."

"You might be right," said Chizu. Then, in a loud voice, she said, "Mother, I bet it's because those dentures don't fit. Why don't you try taking them out?"

"I put in the ones I left next to my pillow last night, so they must be the ones I always wear."

"Even so, they might not be in right," said Chizu. Then, looking at me, she lowered her voice and said, "She just might have taken Oharu-baasan's teeth upstairs last night, eh?"

The old woman grudgingly removed her upper plate. We couldn't tell whose it was just by looking at it. It's not like it has a name on it or anything.

Chizu said, "Can I have a look at it?" She quickly grabbed it, took it into the kitchen and washed it with water and dishwashing liquid. Then she gave Oharu-baasan a signal to come over to where she was standing.

I whispered into Oharu-baasan's ear and got her to go into the kitchen and put the upper plate into her mouth, and—what do you know—it fit her perfectly! Even though she's always saying 'they don't fit so I can't chew things'! Chizu hurriedly went to the bathroom sink and proclaimed in a loud voice, "I found them! I found them!" Then she returned holding another upper plate between her thumb and index finger.

16

After taking Oharu-baasan, who was in a hurry to get back to Tokyo, to Shin Osaka Station, I set off for the first of my appointments at a gallery. From Osaka Station I went down into the underground tunnel system, where I was met by the stench of foul-smelling gases that had accumulated there because of the poor air circulation. I would have thought that by now they would have installed a more modern ventilation system to improve the air quality, but nothing had changed.

Finding it hard to breathe down there, I returned to the surface through an exit next to the Hanshin Department Store. This wasn't where I was going. I needed to get over *there*. I had no idea whether Umeda Shinmichi Street was the same as it used to be. It'd been more than thirty years since I'd lived in Osaka, and even though I occasionally came back, it wasn't always to the same places, so every year when I returned I would get lost; that's why I never learned a surefire way to get to where I was going. To get to the area around Shinmichi—oh yeah, I remembered now—I needed to come out in front of the Sonezaki Police Station.

This time, figuring it would be a surer bet to look at things from the outside, I timidly climbed up onto a pedestrian bridge and crossed a very busy intersection from which great clouds of exhaust fumes billowed up from underfoot, then went into the Hankyu Department Store. Amidst the throngs of people there, I lost my sense of direction again and ended up wandering back and forth for a while.

Long ago—really long ago—when I was only seven or eight and the war had not yet taken a turn for the worse, when there were still sufficient supplies of things—Oharu-baasan would often bring me here. We'd also gone to see the Takarazuka Girls Theater Troupe. Then, too, we had gone through here. Right around here, where I was now standing and almost suffocating, the floor had been completely covered in sparkling clean beige square tiles. Because almost everyone in those days had hobnails on their shoes, they would end up sliding along that floor like they were wearing roller skates, making a lot of clamor as they fell down. On three sides of the building there had been large, open, arched exits, so the ventilation had been good—so good that if you didn't watch out, your hat would be blown off and your skirt would be blown up around your waist. Through the archway on the front of the building you could often see a red streetcar go by. Yes, well, that pedestrian bridge that I had just crossed must be about where the streetcar stop used to be. In those days, I would stand right here and enjoy the smell of vanilla wafting up from the cakes they baked in the food market in the basement of the department store.

Now, I couldn't figure out this area at all. It took a lot of energy just to get away from the throngs of people pushing up against me. I wondered if the population of Osaka had increased so much? Everyone had built homes in the suburbs and the commuter trains were so packed that they needed to add more cars. And that's why they needed to tear down those platforms with the glass-plated roofs over them and make them longer—otherwise there wasn't enough room for the people to stand. Today they extend almost all the way to the next station. They should extend them in this direction, too, I thought, but I guess there wasn't enough land to do that, so they ended up building them in layers, and that's why the ventilation was so bad.

I figured that the Sonezaki Police Station must be just a hop, skip and a jump away, but had no idea how to get there; I couldn't figure out which exit to use. What would happen if there was a big earthquake here, I wondered. I'd end up buried alive with the worthless riffraff all around me. That thought made me panic, and I broke into a cold sweat. How could they create such an impenetrable maze, I fumed.

Even in this state, whenever I saw a male high school student, I stopped and looked for a moment to see if it might be Ichiro.

17

I finally emerged from underground again, having somehow made my way through the maze of tunnels by asking around and overcoming my surprise at discovering that the Sonezaki Police Station now extends down to the subterranean level. The part of the police station that protruded above ground had been transformed from the dirty ocher building of old into a very shiny modern new structure. Against a background of gray skyscrapers, the gingko trees that lined Umeda Shinmichi Street lit up the boulevard with their fluttering cadmium-yellow leaves. Gazing at them as I walked, while also glancing appreciatively at the tall young women in their mod fashions who strode along the avenue, I at last made my way to the Fuji Art Gallery. My appointment was for two o'clock, but I got there about twenty minutes late. No sooner had I pushed open the glass door of the gallery entrance than I heard a shrill voice calling out to me.

"Ooh—it's you! When did you come to Japan?"

Surprised, I turned to see who the voice belonged to. There stood Katayama Chiharu, a woman who had graduated from the same art school as me and subsequently been involved in the Kaibi Kai painters group I was active in; I hadn't seen her in about ten years. She looked a little older, but then again, so did I. She wasn't particularly tall, and as always, her face and hands seemed chubby. She was wearing an expensive-looking suede jacket and jeans and was standing right next to the gallery entrance. Even though she was fifty-eight years old, she had her hair in a style that looked like an Afro from the front but had a little tail hanging down in the back.

She had always been quite energetic and talked in a very loud voice that belied her small stature, so all the other painters—even the guys—were afraid of her and never dared oppose her. The male painters would often say, "Shh, shh," when she entered the room. When she was in school, she'd been a tomboy. She got married before any of the rest of us (though the guys said, "It's hard to believe anyone was willing to marry her") and had two children, but even now, there was a little bit of the hoyden about her.

"Hey, Meg—it's been a while!" she said, her voice tinged with nostalgia as she came towards me.

I didn't know how to respond. You see, I had come to the gallery with a vague hope of entering into a contract to sell my paintings. So, in a manner of speaking, it was like having a business rival there ahead of me. Moreover, since I live abroad, my time in Japan is limited, which meant Chiharu was at a distinct advantage, living in the area as she did and undoubtedly being well-informed of the situation in Japan's—or should I say Kansai's—art world. And now that I was here, I obviously couldn't ask her how I might be able to promote myself to this gallery either.

"Well, well, well, well, Chiharu," I said, forcing myself to put some enthusiasm into my voice. "I never expected to run into you here . . . How're you doing?"

"Oh, not bad, I guess. If you've got some time, let's go to a coffee shop somewhere around here and talk."

"Sure. Can you wait just a little bit? I'm supposed to meet someone from the gallery. Could you hold on for an hour—no—thirty minutes or so?"

"Of course I'll wait—for a visitor from so far away! I don't have to worry about getting home; I've turned the household over to my son's wife, and as for my husband, he's retired and is just *sodai gomi*," she said breezily.

"*Sodai gomi*? What's that?" I asked, imagining that it was written with the Chinese characters for "ancestors' relish." "Is that the name of some kind of tea or confection or something? It's a very fancy name, anyway."

"You don't know what that means? That's what we call over-size garbage like furniture and electrical appliances. These days, retired husbands get called that, too. In both cases, even when we're ready to dump them, we can't get rid of them very easily. You really don't know anything about what's happening in Japan now, do you?"

What a nasty expression! I was shocked. And yet, up until now, Japanese women have been treated even worse than *sodai gomi*, I thought. Now that they've grown older, they've got more male hormones than female hormones and they're physically stronger, so perhaps they're just getting their revenge.

"Of course not. I'm almost like a foreigner. Especially when it comes to the latest popular expressions—there's no way I could know what they mean."

"Yeah, well, do what you have to do quick and then come join me."

I fidgeted the whole time I was with the gallery manager—a man of about forty-five who looked very smart in his Armani suit and without ever saying it, made it clear that he believed "Art is business." Disgusted with myself for not knowing which was more important—a solo show or a friend—I could not compose myself as I talked and showed my slides, so I left the gallery fairly quickly. Since the manager had to look over the gallery's own schedule before deciding whether or not to let me show my work there, he politely asked me to let him send his answer to me after I'd returned to the States.

Katayama Chiharu stands only a little taller than my shoulders, but as we walked along Umeda Shinmichi Street, making our way through the crowds of people, she spoke in a loud voice. "*Homma ni*—what have you been up to?" She wasn't shy about anything—even I looked timid in comparison. And her voice really carried. We entered her favorite establishment—a coffee shop cum snack bar with a nice atmosphere. Simon and Garfunkel's "Mrs. Robinson" was playing: "A nation turns its lonely eyes to you (woo woo woo) . . ."

As soon as we sat down at a table, she said, "Say, did you know that Koyama-Sensei passed away?"

I was stunned. A teacher who was so careful about his health—dead? "When?"

"Late last year."

That really upset me. Whenever I came back to Japan (although I wasn't able to return while my kids were still at home, so I really only came back here after I'd been living in the States for twenty years), the first person I went to see was Koyama-Sensei. After that first visit, I had always made it a point to go and see him, but last spring, even though I'd been in his neighborhood, I hadn't dropped in on him, nor had I telephoned, and now I regretted it.

He always used to say that painters need to live long lives. A painter who is still alive after the other painters of his generation have all died will be regarded as a great painter, you see—no matter what kind of works he paints, because critics don't really understand much at all, he would explain. I suppose he was just kidding, but then again, when you think about it, he wasn't a serious artist.

The two of us had taken Koyama-Sensei's class while we were at the art school, and even after we graduated he still gave us instruction. He was about twenty years older than us and already married, but he had come back to Japan before the war from Belle Epoque France and was not only handsome, but well-versed in Western fashion, so he was very popular with the ladies, and his classes were always full—with only female students.

After a period of silence, I said, "Wow. I thought he . . . would live a lot longer." It made me sad. A person I knew, a person I'd felt affection for and had been close to had disappeared.

"His wife died last April; after that, he had three housemaids take turns coming and taking care of him."

"Oh? What's Makino-san doing? I heard from Shiono-san, who's living in Los Angeles now, that even when his wife was alive, Makino-san would always go with him to Tokyo for the opening of the Tokyo-Ten Art Exhibition. Didn't she move in with him the moment his wife died?"

Just like in the old days, Chiharu gulped down the beer that had been put out for us, then excitedly pounded the glass back down the table and shouted, "No way! Sensei was the one who was being taken advantage of."

The coffee shop suddenly went quiet. But maybe it just seemed like that because the background music had stopped.

"Listen, can you keep it down a little?" I blurted out.

"What? Is somebody we know here?" she said, surveying our surroundings.

"No, no one," I answered, though I don't know anybody that

she knows.

Makino-san was a very rich woman who had stood high in Koyama-Sensei's favor. Up until last year, she had shamelessly submitted work that Koyama-Sensei had painted for her to the Kaibi Kai competition every year, and her works had been chosen to be included in the Exhibition starting from the same year that ours had, so by now, she no longer needed to push or be pushed—her position as a group member was solid, and the relationship between the two of them was well-known even within the Kaibi Kai, Chiharu told me.

The coffee shop's background music system switched to wonderful old chansons by Yves Montand. Why, he was singing "*Clémentine*"!

Un peu beaucoup et même à la folie
La première fois qu'on aime comme c'est joli
Les amours enfantines
Quels secrets merveilleux
Je vois toujours briller les yeux
De Clémentine, de Clémentine

Whenever I hear his gentle, sweet voice singing this melody, no matter where I am, I'm always in the mood for love—even though I don't have a lover. I feel like youth has returned to me. Not many songs can make me feel this way. The man I've been married to for thirty years can't do this for me. Not even Montand himself—whom I last saw, his face all wrinkled, from an orchestra seat in the Greek Theater in Los Angeles—can do this. Only this voice can make me feel this way. It doesn't belong here with Chiharu talking—the two are like oil and water. It seems to me that this song makes everything ugly about humanity melt away.

Perhaps because I was so silent, wrapped up in my own little fantasies, Chiharu raised her voice again and said, "Makino-san is the one who had the upper hand. Hey, are you listening to me? Makino-san was the one who had the upper hand, and when Sensei was left alone and helpless, she didn't care enough about him to move in with him and take care of him. It was Sensei who put everything he had into their relationship—not the other way around. He wasn't a good judge of character, and he ended up losing all of his good students—that is, the ones who were seriously trying to paint."

"Who are you talking about? Who are the ones who were seriously trying to paint?"

"The three women he disliked were all serious, I think."

"And who, pray tell, are those three women?"

"Huh? You don't know?"

"One of them is you, I suppose. And then there's Shiono-san, who's living in Los Angeles now. I can figure out that much, but who's the other one?"

"You don't know?"

"No, I don't know. I have no idea who it is."

"Ha! You're so easygoing! It's you, of course!"

"No! I thought he liked me."

"Well, aren't you lucky! To be unaware of the fact that you've been disliked all these years. People like you who made a leap of faith and began abstract painting—Koyama-Sensei hated them. There were just three of us who did that: ignored his advice and took up abstract painting."

"Oh. I never knew that."

I'd had no idea that I was disliked, but even if Koyama-Sensei had favored me, I couldn't have been satisfied with him and would have gone to America anyway. Like the rest of Japanese society, I had been greatly influenced by the Western ideas that flooded into the country right after the end of the war. At that time, I believed originality was the essence of art and that to be original you had to do something different from what others were doing. I hated going to exhibitions of traditional Japanese paintings, so-called Nihonga-style, and seeing clusters of similar works where you could easily tell which were painted by the teacher and which by his disciples. Now that I'm older, I understand that this is part of the learning process and looked strange only because all these copycat works were on display simultaneously. The same thing happens everywhere. The system of apprenticeship exists in Europe, too. Until they master the secrets of painting, all artists imitate their teacher. Then once they have made the techniques their own, they paint to express themselves. The end is the same for all. I just didn't realize that when I was young.

Even so, I was really turned off by Japanese art circles, where critical acclaim did not go to unique works created by artists who had built on the techniques they'd mastered, but instead, was awarded to paintings that imitated the works of famous artists and could clearly be labeled as Cezanne-like or Gauguin-like.

In those days, I was trying to devise techniques to allow me to paint Nihonga-style works in oils. I would dissolve paint in turpentine to make it thin enough to put a wash of color on the canvas. Then, before it had dried, I would get another color on my brush and allow a drop or two to fall onto the wet surface. Koyama-Sensei was dead set against my doing this.

"Listen—that has too little form. It's weak. If nobody else does it, you shouldn't do it either."

"This is supposed to be abstract," I tried to argue.

That's when I went to the American Culture Center and

looked at books showing what artists in America were producing: paintings by Mondrian, Ernst, Pollock, Rothko and de Kooning, as well as the works of sculptress Louise Nevelson. They were all doing exactly as they pleased.

"Koyama-Sensei was completely enamored of that worthless bum who didn't paint and just used him to try to finagle status for herself, and that's why he ended up all alone in the end," Chiharu reasoned. "Because Makino-san was there, the rest of us wouldn't go near him. If he'd treated those of us who were serious about painting better, I think we all would have taken care of him a little. He once told me that his life would probably have been much more interesting if he'd married the woman he brought back from France with him. I wonder why he was afraid of his wife?"

"I'm sure it was because her family was rich," I answered. "Do you know any other painters who were able to build a house like that right after the war? Of course, there were artists who had nice houses that hadn't been burned down during the air raids, but besides them . . . And don't you think that the reason he fell for Makino-san was also at least partly because her relatives and business associates bought his paintings? I mean, I think he thought of women painters as people he could use and that it was not a problem if their paintings were little more than a hobby. But you know, Shiono-san told me that in Los Angeles she had met someone from a gallery in Kyoto that handles Makino-san's paintings."

"Oh, yeah. That guy. The works she sells aren't oil paintings. She had to get Koyama-Sensei to do her oil paintings for her. But in watercolor, she painted a number of pictures that were exactly the same—kind of like a coloring book—and she sells those. For ¥100,000 each. I guess she gets companies that do business with her brother's company to buy them."

"Really?" I was so engrossed in her story that I forgot to drink my beer. But at the same time, I felt strongly that this was entertaining only because I was not directly involved, and I had absolutely no desire to get pulled back into this world.

Chiharu took a bite of her sandwich and a drink of beer, then said, "The Kansai Kaibi Kai is finished. We've all grown old. Yas-san acts like he's the general manager and Bun-chan can't stand up to him, so it's really gone downhill."

"Well, how about the Tokyo Kaibi Kai?"

"Oh, one of the members got the Japan Art Academy Award. They say it's the first time in Kaibi Kai history. But you know, the winner is chosen by the members of the Art Academy. I hear the guy who got the prize actually paid ten million yen to each member of the Academy."

"You're kidding! That kind of thing really happens? That much money! They take it without any qualms? I don't have that kind of money, but even if I did, I'd use it for myself, not for that."

"I hear that his gallery paid half of it."

"Why?"

"Well, the price of your paintings goes up if you win the Art Academy Award."

"Listen, getting back to Makino-san. With Koyama-Sensei dead, she doesn't have anyone to make paintings for her, does she?"

"Oh, that reminds me: there's a Kaibi Kai meeting the day after tomorrow starting at six in the evening. It's the first time we're getting together since Koyama-Sensei died. Everyone's just dying to find out what will happen to Makino-san, so I'm sure there'll be a lot of people there. Everyone'll want to see her get what she's got coming to her now that she doesn't have someone standing up for her anymore. That'll be something to see. Want to come?"

"Well . . ." I said noncommittally, since this invitation had come totally out of the blue.

"You gotta come! This kind of thing doesn't happen every day. We never have meetings while you're back in Japan." She took a breath, then moved in to finalize the matter. "You won't know the way, so why don't we meet at Hankyu Umeda Station, in front of the second-floor wicket, at five thirty. Where are you staying?"

"Shukugawa. At my sister's place."

"I'm living in Takarazuka now, so Hankyu Umeda is perfect for both of us."

What can I say? Was the whole Kaibi Kai like this? I was starting to think that even though it was just a small group, it was a really frightening community with lots of bullying going on, but my curiosity was piqued so I decided to go.

18

We entered a room like the hall of a small school. A large rectangular table had been set up against one wall, and on it was an array of hors d'oeuvres, beer and soft drinks. People were sitting and standing around the room talking, holding paper cups into which they had poured the drink of their choice. Many young men and women appeared to be painters and sculptors: some wore berets, others had punk hair or the wild wavy hair style known as *sauvage*; some had purple hair and others, blond or even pink hair—there was quite a variety. I was reminded of myself in my youth and felt a wave of nostalgia sweep over me. Compared to then, young people today certainly have more creativity and can more or less dress as they like.

About the only person I knew was Yas-san, who was sitting in the front of the room wearing a dark brown corduroy jacket. He was a very competitive person who had always succeeded in getting good placement for his paintings in our exhibitions in the Tennoji Art Museum—that is, he got them hung next to paintings by the chairman of the group or works by painters who were famous in Tokyo. I, on the other hand, had always wandered around and finally ended up getting my painting

hung near the exit. Of course, Yas-san laudably always volun-
teered to serve as the person in charge of arranging the works—
complaining all the while that it was a pain because you had to
get there early in the morning, but his hidden agenda was to
ensure that his entry was well-placed. His paintings were poin-
tillist works that looked just like Seurat's. He had no originality
whatsoever.

Of course, there had been a few times when leaders of our
group, such as Koyama-Sensei and Honda-Sensei, had chewed
Yas-san out when they came and found that their paintings
were not in the central room of the exhibition hall, but still, it
was this kind of politics rather than the real value of the paintings that held sway, so the ordinary people who came to see
the exhibitions were deceived about the relative worth of the
displayed works. At times like that, there was no such thing as
camaraderie among fellow artists. The men quickly took the
best places as a matter of course.

Yas-san was about sixty-two years old now. He had aged; he
was a bit chubbier than before, and his complexion had grown
ruddy. Since his was the only face I recognized, I figured I should
say hello. I went over and greeted him, giving my family name,
Nakayama, but he looked at me like he hadn't the slightest idea
who I was. Taken aback, I decided to call Katayama Chiharu
over to help me and went over to where she was standing.

"He's so strange, isn't he?" she complained. "Your name
came up just at the last meeting. You see, we'd heard that you'd
had a solo show in New York and everyone was talking about
how amazing that was. Then Yas-san said, '*Homma kai naa*' like
he didn't believe it, and with a pinched look on his face, added
that you were really scary. It's just sour grapes. He doesn't want
to acknowledge your success, so he's pretending not to know
you."

Just then, I recalled something Okada Kenzo once told me. It was just after we'd moved to New York, and there weren't very many Japanese people living there at the time, so when I heard that the famous Japanese artist was living in the apartment next door to us, I went to visit him. He told me that he belonged to the Nika Association of artists in Japan and complained that just around the time he was getting critical acclaim in America for paintings based on traditional Japanese patterns, whenever he was back in Japan and happened to attend a party for painters, they were so caught up in their jealousy of him that they refused to talk to him.

Chiharu accompanied me as I went back to where Yas-san was sitting and said in her screechy voice,

"Hey, look who's here—it's Meg, who went to live in America. I can't believe you can't remember someone this famous! I thought you were always afraid of her."

Yas-san scratched his head and, with a pinched expression on his face, said, "Oh—sorry; I didn't recognize you. I've been so busy running this group, how could I be expected to remember someone from so long ago? But now that I think of it, you're just like Chiharu—there's no stopping you once you get talking. I'm getting out of here." As he spoke, he looked over to one side and then hurried off in that direction.

There, an old man—he must have been about eighty-eight years old—wearing glasses and barely able to walk, was being led into the room on the arm of his elderly wife.

"Honda-Sensei," Yas-san yelled into the old man's right ear. "Thank you so much for going out of your way to come so far to attend this meeting today. How are you?"

This was Honda-san! How he'd changed! At the time when I'd first had a work accepted for inclusion in a Kaibi Kai exhibition, he'd been bustling about in his role as master of ceremonies—the job that Yas-san was now handling—and had been quite full of himself because his illustrations were often used in both the local and national newspapers.

Yas-san climbed onto the low stage, so Chiharu and I returned to our seats. After adjusting the height of the mike, Yas-san addressed the group.

"Good evening, everyone. I'd like to open the annual social meeting of the Kansai Chapter of Kaibi Kai. To start with, we'd like to hear a few words from a leader of the art world and one of our most senior members, Honda-Sensei."

He quickly came down off the dais and, taking Honda-Sensei's arm, slowly and carefully helped him up onto the platform.

"I think he needs a chair," he said, instructing a young man who was sitting just in front of the dais to bring one. Then he lowered the mike again.

Honda-san began to talk in a very faint voice that was quite hard to hear; what's worse, he seemed to have phlegm in his throat. Even though he was using the mike, I don't think the people in the back of the room could have heard anything.

"Tha-ank yo-u for that wonderful introductio-n," he began, prolonging the vowels at the end of each phrase as he paused for breath—or was it to think? "Young Yasuda-kun asked me to say a few wo-rds to you today, so, although I'm not in the best of health, I decided to co-ome." He coughed a couple of times, then continued. "I'm happy to say that the Kansai Chapter of Kaibi Kai is doing well . . . At last, membership is u-p! The number of members whose works are accepted for exhibit is u-p! This year, young Koyama-kun has returned from Tokyo-u, and he said that they had a very hard time judging this yea-r, as there were ma-ny excellent submissio-ns, but that ten artists from Kansai had their work accepted for exhibition for the first ti-me, which is extre-mely good ne-ws."

A young man behind me asked the woman sitting next to him, "Who is 'Koyama-kun'? Isn't that the guy who died last year? 'Ten artists had their works accepted for the first time'? Did that many pass?"

"Also, just the other day, young Yamamoto-kun ca-me back ho-me to Japan from Fra-nce on the NYK Line steamer Chi-chibu-ma-ru. I look for-ward to seeing what kind of pai-ntings he'll create after his studies in the We-st. In France, the Post Impressionists are just at the hei-ght of their popularit-y, so he says he really learned a lo-t. Ah, ah, ah. He said he studie-d at the Lhote Studio in Pa-ris. He told me that he was fri-ghtened because it lo-oks as if war is about to break ou-t in Europe, and that's why- he came back ho-me."

I couldn't understand half of what he was saying, so I looked over at Chiharu, who was sitting next to me. She looked like she was about to burst out laughing.

"Huh? What's he saying? What a weird talk! He's in another time period," complained the young man sitting behind me.

"What a waste of time—listening to a senile old fart like that," came a stage whisper from a man sitting a little further back.

Since he was almost deaf, the speaker continued his talk unperturbed.

At last, Honda Sensei finished and came down from the dais. As he was being led out the door by his wife, Yas-san returned to the platform and nonchalantly said, "*Homma ni*, that was pointless—a foolish talk that made no sense whatsoever. What a waste of your time."

I was dumbfounded. According to Chiharu, all the other painters who I had known when I was living in Japan had died. Among those who might be called great, only Honda Sensei was still alive, so it seemed they always had him come to the annual social meeting.

"Honda Sensei had heart surgery," Chiharu explained. "They fixed his heart but during the operation, one of his veins was cut and he lost his hearing. He has a hearing aid but apparently it howls a lot, so he doesn't use it most of the time. And, you know, what he says is totally incoherent, so you go crazy listening to him. All the names he mentioned just now were painters from a lo-o-o-ng time ago, so none of the young guys here would know who they were. He was talking about stuff that happened before World War II or during the Post-Impressionist Period—utter nonsense, wasn't it?"

Then she continued in a whisper: "On top of that, Yas-san always has Honda-san talk and then right afterwards, in front of everybody, he says, 'what a fool, giving such a pointless talk.' You want to know why? Because when he was young, he was bullied really badly by Honda Sensei. So now it's payback time. Anybody would get fed up listening to such nonsense even once, but he has him do the same thing every year and then abuses him afterward so that he can get even for what he did years ago. And he gets away with it because Honda Sensei can't hear him!"

"What happened to Bun-chan?" I asked, suddenly reminded of another male painter who was about the same age as Yas-san and had enjoyed a similar level of success.

"Oh, he's been sick a lot. And Shono-san died last year. That's why only Yas-san is left to run this group. That man really looks down on women and says they can't paint. And yet, when he needs to decide an important matter for the Kaibi Kai, he'll come to me and say, 'Hey, Chiharu, can you give me some advice?' I'll tell him something like, 'Are you kidding? Who's the one who's always saying that women are silly? I'm a woman,

so I can't possibly give you advice on such an important matter.'
You know what he has the nerve to say then? 'I don't think of
you as a woman.' I think that's much worse—it's like he's not
recognizing women's rights at all."

"Hey, is Makino-san here?" I asked, surveying the hall.

Chiharu joined me in scanning the crowd. Turning back to
me, she said, "It doesn't look like it. She must have been too
scared to show up."

When I'm talking with Chiharu, I start feeling really nostalgic
about the past. I get happy just thinking about what it would be
like to come back to Japan at some point and settle down again
in the Kansai area, joking around with my friends and speaking
in Kansai-ben to my heart's content.

Yet I know I can't live in Japan. Ken is hospitalized, a ward
of the state, so we'll have to live in California for the rest of our
lives. Who else could stand up for his rights? Who knows how
long that state hospital will be there? And we don't want to push
this responsibility off onto John at this point. We don't want to
burden him with this, although eventually, it will be his burden
to bear.

Also, prices in Japan are high, so we couldn't afford to buy a
house here. And most of the painters I know have died. On top
of that, from what Chiharu says, I can see that art circles in this
country have not changed much over the years. I tell myself that
it would not be good for my mental health to get caught up in
this world again.

All the same, I felt Kansai pulling on my heartstrings as I
left for Tokyo. We still had no idea where Ichiro was. He hadn't
called Oharu-baasan either.

During my last two days in Japan before returning to America, in the middle of packing my things, I took the time to contact two Christian schoolmates of mine who had both moved up to Tokyo when their husbands had been transferred there, and asked them to see if they could find some Protestant churches near Oharu-baasan's retirement home. I arranged for them to give the addresses to my brother Yoshio and asked him to talk with Oharu-baasan about which one she'd like to go to. Having taken care of that little bit of family business, I returned to the States.

After I got back, John stayed in California for another two days, and then he returned to Japan.

19

Two months later I got a call from John saying that Ichiro was staying with him. I thought I must be dreaming. He told me Ichiro was really enjoying himself. Apparently, the boy had called Oharu-baasan and asked for John's phone number. It turned out that Ichiro had a friend in high school who'd moved up to Tokyo with his parents; he was a rather unusual kid in that he'd always dreamed of being a chef. According to John, Ichiro had been really jealous of him because his parents were supporting him in following his dream. That was one of the reasons he'd run away. Another was probably that he'd helped his cousin Shimpei and seen firsthand that he was doing fine as a chef with his own restaurant.

Ichiro intended to enroll in the same cooking school as his friend, so he'd been staying at the friend's house for a month. Feeling uncomfortable about freeloading for so long, however, he decided he should rent a cheap apartment for himself and go to school from there. So now he was staying at John's place to learn about what it was like to be independent.

Well, John and Ichiro are cousins, so for John, it was kind of like suddenly having a younger brother around; it would probably be a very good experience for him, since his real younger brother can't even talk. Ichiro said he would earn his rent by working part-time. And as for food, he figured that since he's going to cooking school, he'll probably get something to eat every day.

According to John, Chizu was really grateful to him. She'd come up to Tokyo recently and met with John and Ichiro and, unbeknownst to Tatsuo, had given her son some money to pay John for his living expenses.

After she'd gone home, Ichiro apparently told John, "My mom's not at all mad at me for running away; she accepts my decision and says that I can do what I want as long as I take responsibility for it. My dad's another story, though—she says he's still furious with me. What's worse, even though I'm here imposing on you, he has this strange idea that the reason I'm not coming back home is because you have a bad influence on me. I'm really sorry about that. My mom's really mad at my dad for thinking that way."

Then John told me, "Uncle Tatsuo can think whatever he wants—it doesn't bother me a bit. It's not like I'm ever going to need something from him anyway. He's the embodiment of ego. He gets mad when his son won't do what he wants and then shifts the blame onto me. He doesn't see that it's his fault."

That was when I realized that Tatsuo was the type of person who curried favor with people he thought would be able to help him get ahead and treated everyone else—those younger than him and people without any particular status—as if they were worms. He was always frantically trying to sell himself at conferences and universities in hopes of getting a Nobel prize, yet he had transferred his own lack of recognition onto John, who was somewhat of an outsider in Japanese society. I mean, Tatsuo wanted to get acclaim from abroad, but was unwilling to accept someone who came from another country and was a little different from him. It was probably this contradiction that made the whole situation worse.

Nonetheless, Chizu was already being forced to take care of Tatsuo's mother rather than her own, and it appeared that this was quite difficult. Since it was Tatsuo's mother, he really should have been the one caring for her. If he had been aware of that, perhaps he would have understood Ichiro's problems better, too. I hinted at such things in a letter I wrote to Chizu.

In her reply she said, "I am so grateful to John for all his help. Now that Ichiro has someone on his side, he feels hopeful about the future and sometimes calls me on days when Tatsuo teaches at the university. But you know, you don't understand the way things are in Japan, so there's no way I can explain to you how people interact here. In Japan even now, people take it for granted that a wife will take care of her mother-in-law."

Later on, a strange thing happened. Even though I'd taken time out of my busy schedule and troubled my friends with my request to get the addresses of some local churches, Oharu-baasan told my brother and his wife, "You know, I don't want you to hold my funeral in a Christian church. I haven't been baptized." My older brother Yoshio told me this during a phone conversation.

"What? And after putting everyone out like that!"

"Yeah, well, that's why I told you Oharu-baasan has been running around in circles her whole life. We're always being jerked around by her, you know."

"Sorry about that," I said, apologizing to my brother.

"So now, you know, she says she wants a Buddhist funeral and she wants to be buried in a grave next to Grandpa's."

"Hmm. Is she starting to get senile?" I asked.

"I have no idea," responded Yoshio.

It suddenly occurred to me that at her age, it might have seemed really depressing to Oharu-baasan to have to go to a new place and start up new relationships, so it just may have felt easier to say she wasn't a Christian.

A month later, on an April day that was as hot as summer here, I suddenly got a call from John, who asked, "Is it true that you can't have a Jewish funeral unless you covert to Judaism?"

"I should think so. Why, are you planning on becoming Jewish?"

"No—that's not what this is about. I suddenly got a call from Grandma Oharu, and she asked me if Jewish funerals are simple. I told her I didn't know."

What on earth? Now it's Judaism? Whoa! I'm completely lost. Has Oharu-baasan started running around in circles again? If so, then everything becomes a matter of timing—of when her running in circles stops. And when her breathing stops. Whatever religion she wants to be at that moment in time is the one we should rely on for her funeral, but that doesn't mean we'll know what's really in her heart. After the onset of senility, there's no way to know for sure. So we'll just have to let her take her pick.

In that way, Japan is quite convenient. People there think nothing of having a Christian wedding and a Buddhist funeral. In the West, that kind of thing would be unthinkable and might even give rise to bloodshed.

To me, a human being is little more than a grain of sand, pushed along by the great tide of life—flow, ebb, recede—a cycle that will go on, with me or without, with Oharu-baasan or . . . not, so none of this really makes any difference.

All the same, I'm glad that for now, we're just talking about her funeral rather than actually making arrangements for it.

1001 Fires Raging

"A riot is the language of the unheard."
Martin Luther King, Jr.

"Color is not a human or a personal reality;
it is a political reality."
James Baldwin

1

April 29, 1992

Yu slid open her studio glass doors; the gentle, salty breeze felt good against her cheek. There was the ocean, the smoggy blue sky. On the hazy horizon, Catalina Island was barely visible beyond water dotted by yachts' white sails. There wasn't even a hot Santa Ana wind sweeping down from the mountains to disturb this sunny April afternoon in Southern California. The faint chirping of birds pecking at insects on trees in the garden swelled, then the flock took flight, the thin branches of the Satsuma tangerine tree swaying as they went.

The departing birds were bushtits, similar to a bush warbler, only smaller. A flock of about fifty of them regularly came to the yard. They gathered under the foliage in the garden, although they were easy to miss because they were the same color as the leaves. A few always lingered, flying away after the rest. Yu watched the stragglers, then turned her attention to the unfinished drawing on her desk. "I've got to finish this today," she said to herself in Japanese, rolling up the sleeves on her white sweatshirt and easing up the knees on her khaki-colored cotton pants as she sat down on her swivel chair.

But she was again distracted by the garden; she noticed the tangerines were early this year—small green fruit beginning to develop on the branches of the Satsuma tangerine tree, which she had planted ten years earlier. The tree was a dwarf, about three feet tall, and normally at this time of year it was bedecked with tiny white flowers. In winter, it bore sweet, golden little fruit.

The name suggested that this variety originally came from the Satsuma area of Kyushu in Japan. Yu had never seen this kind of mandarin orange in the Kansai area of Japan where she'd grown up, but she figured that long ago, the seeds had been secreted into the country in an immigrant's luggage or pocket. How amazing to be able to take root in a desert like this, Yu thought. Its story reminded her of her own life's journey, so the tree had a special place in Yu's heart.

She would use the orange in her design, she decided: flattened round green fruit and leaves alternating in a vertical line against a white background. Yu picked up the sketchbook lying open at her side and began drawing the composition in pencil.

"No, not green oranges," she told herself. "Yellow and orange fruit, in contrast to the green leaves in between them."

She wrote down in her sketchbook the names of the colors she intended to use. Since she was the only one in her family who spoke Japanese, Yu had long been in the habit of talking to herself and telling herself what to do in her native tongue. And naturally, she used the dialect of the place where she'd grown up: Osaka.

Recently, Yu had started receiving requests to make textile designs here in Los Angeles. She had done this kind of work years ago, but once she'd had two daughters with her spouse

Bob, a WASP, she'd been too busy taking care of the children and doing the housework to continue her career. Having married rather late, Yu was past fifty before her girls set off for colleges on the East Coast.

While she had been raising her daughters, she sometimes became despondent at the prospect of spending the rest of her life as a housewife. She might not have felt that way if she hadn't had a career in textile design decades ago, just after she'd arrived in the States from Japan and was living in New York. She had made a living for herself in this rather difficult field then. But when she tried to start up again in Los Angeles after her long hiatus and without contacts in the industry, she'd pretty much had to start all over again. It had been a gradual climb back into her profession but she felt like she had finally reestablished herself at age sixty-one.

Yu's husband Bob was not very easy to deal with. Yu felt that men of his age—sixty-five—tended to be quite old-fashioned, even in America. It was true that American society was more open to women in many respects. American women had begun their march toward liberation earlier, so the men here had been pushed further and would no longer publicly argue about women's rights. These days it was considered bad form to publicly resist the trend toward gender equality too much, so more men were just keeping their mouths shut about it. All the same, Yu observed, no one wants to lose power once they've got it, so she suspected that in their hearts, men everywhere looked back fondly on the days when they had the upper hand.

Although Japan and America were at different stages in terms of social evolution, Yu's experience as a Japanese person who had lived in America for many years had led her to think that people's attitudes adjusted at the same slow pace everywhere. Thus, she felt that the degree of old-fashioned thinking displayed by an American sixty-five year-old man would probably be roughly equal to his Japanese counterpart.

When it came to minorities, Bob was more understanding than most, since he was married to Yu. None of his upper middle-class friends had anything to do with anyone from a minority group. The only non-WASPs they encountered regularly were those they employed, such as the Mexicans who came to clean their homes, the elderly Japanese-Americans and Mexicans who took care of their gardens, and the Koreans who painted houses. They paid lip service to the elimination of discrimination, but inwardly they wondered why they had to give up their power, and were not truly interested in minority rights. Bob, on the other hand, by virtue of living with the highly vocal Yu, was exposed to a constant stream of complaints about a range of minority issues on a daily basis. He was at least aware that this was still a real issue.

Whenever an issue involving two different races defied all conventional logic or caused tension for no discernible reason, Yu would claim that this was because of prejudice. Yet, as a member of the dominant ethnic group, Bob would always write off her complaints as paranoid delusions and thus manage to avoid looking at things her way. This made Yu think that even between a married couple, unless you were blessed with tremendous powers of imagination, there were a lot of things that you just couldn't understand unless you actually tried on your spouse's skin.

Yu had already been over fifty by the time their children had left the nest. When she started calling around to see if she could get back into textile design again, Bob had supported her, commenting, "It's good for women to have a job; it gives you a larger perspective."

"Oh, how understanding!" she'd replied. "I would never

have thought you'd be so liberal. Thank you! Thank you! Tell your friends I'm looking for work."

"My friends aren't in graphic design; they're copywriters. And even graphics is not the same as textiles. If I meet someone who does graphic design, I'll mention it, but I'm not sure it will help."

Since Bob had encouraged her to find work, Yu had figured that he'd surely contribute to the housework. Putting the designs she'd made years ago in a large folding portfolio, she'd starting going out frequently to try to find an agent.

One day, she lost track of the time and got stuck in rush-hour traffic. Hollywood's Sunset Boulevard was backed up, so it was seven thirty and already dark when she finally reached home. On her way up to her studio to put away her portfolio, Yu passed the living room. The lights were on and Bob was sitting there on the sofa reading the newspaper.

"Did you get something ready for supper?" Yu asked expectantly.

"What are you talking about? You're not bringing in any money yet. The person bringing home the bacon should get cut a little slack. I think you should handle the housework until you have an income of your own," he said without looking up from the newspaper.

When she heard those words, Yu's round face, which had been tanned by the southern Californian sun, suddenly went tense and her eyes narrowed. Putting the heavy portfolio down on the floor, and then both hands on her hips, she yelled, "Am I your slave? Whose children did I spend more than twenty years raising? Didn't I have an income in New York before we got married, and—before the girls were born—even after we got married? And who was it that was in favor of my getting a job just the other day? So even while I'm just looking for work, if I don't get a little help . . . At least when I get home late, you could get dinner ready. If you won't do that, then from now, I'm going to charge you every time I clean."

When she finished spitting that out, Yu picked up her portfolio from the floor with her right hand, but, apparently unsatisfied, she just stood there like that and continued her tirade.

"And I'll charge you retroactively for raising the girls. That's a total of twenty years. When they were little, I had to take care of them twelve hours a day. There were two of them, so that's twice as much. Adults at that time got seven dollars an hour for babysitting, so that's, uhmm, seven times twelve—eighty-four dollars. I was watching two at the same time, so that's a hundred and sixty dollars. Per day, okay? So for a year, you'd have to multiply it by three hundred sixty-five. Uhmm, could you give me a pencil and paper?"

"All right. I got it. I got it," sighed Bob, raising his bushy eyebrows and trying to calm her down while sounding as if he were thinking, "Here we go again."

"Calculated like that, my income would be nothing to stick your nose up at. You're like someone straight out of the Victorian era. You're not logical. How many years did I have to stand in the wings, grinding my teeth, until the girls went off to college?"

Yu was not a natural when it came to housework. All the same, when the girls had been little, she took care of things efficiently and had at least given a nod to nutrition in preparing meals. However, from about the time her daughters had left home to go to college, Bob had developed heart disease and she'd had to learn how to cook fat-free, low-cholesterol foods. On top of that, Yu was not good at multitasking. She was the type of person who, when she got absorbed in one thing, would completely forget about everything else. In addition, Bob was a freelance copywriter, so he was free to do his work at whatever time he set for himself. If he would take charge of at least half of the housework, Yu felt she would be able to make up for lost time and work at a leisurely pace. Then as she neared the end of her life, she would finally be able to enjoy life a little.

That had been almost ten years ago. Although Yu still complained about inequality, they had gotten to the point where they were managing somehow.

2

Two days earlier, Yu had gone to the office of an agent named Fiona in the Wilshire district to ask about the design samples she had given her a while back and see if Fiona could get her some new orders. Fiona's office was situated in an elegant pink two-story building decorated with a white stucco pattern shaped like the Acanthus leaves that appeared on the top of Corinthian columns in ancient Greek architecture. Yu went up to the second floor and opened the door at the top of the stairs. Inside, a young woman she had never seen before—the secretary or receptionist, perhaps—was sitting and chewing gum noisily. She must have been hired recently. She had on a blouse with the neck opened wide enough to show off a great deal of her pale skin, which contrasted with her red nail polish. She continued to file her nails as she raised her eyes to look at Yu with suspicion, the whites of her large blue eyes clearly visible as she stared at Yu's face.

It seemed that there were no other visitors. The next room, which was Fiona's, was also quiet.

"What do you want?" the young woman asked, as if she were talking to an errand boy.

"You must be new. Please tell Fiona that Yu is here."

"Oh, did you have an appointment?" the young woman asked as she stretched out her neck in the direction of the schedule on her desk and looked it over.

"When I called Fiona yesterday I said I would stop by today," Yu said sullenly.

The girl twisted her body as she stood up and then, swaying her large derriere wrapped in very tight jeans, leisurely made her way into the next room.

When she came back out, the girl waved Yu in with her hand. "She says just ten minutes."

Yu could not tell if Fiona had actually said that.

When she opened the door, she saw Fiona sitting at a large desk right in the middle of the spacious room. Ten fresh-looking yellow roses were casually arranged in a cut glass vase on her desk. Behind her, there were large French windows with white lace curtains. Both the right and left walls were fitted with shelves painted in white enamel. The shelves held designs drawn on large sheets of paper and were subdivided into compartments so that the designs could be filed according to category.

"Hi Fiona! How are you?" said Yu in a loud voice as she closed the door.

Fiona was a hefty woman who appeared to be about fifty years old, with thick hair dyed to an unnaturally ocher-brown wound up on top of her head with a black-lacquered chopstick stuck in it. A wide, finely crafted gold necklace hung on her white, nearly translucent skin, running along the round neckline of the Egyptian-style garment that draped her plump body and appeared to be more of a robe than a dress. Her oval face was freckled, her nose not particularly large, her big round eyes accented by black eyeliner and blue eye shadow on the upper lid, reminding Yu of the bust of Nefertiti she had seen in a photo book of great works of art. Fiona seemed to be in an

Egyptian mood today. Depending upon how she was feeling, she would dress up in clothes that echoed various national costumes—Spanish or Indian, perhaps—although come to think of it, Yu had never seen her in a kimono. She sat with her chair turned to one side, her right elbow resting on her desk, looking at the design she held in her right hand.

"Oh, Yu. How are you doing?" As she spoke, she turned the design she had been looking at face down on her desk, stood up and came over to Yu to shake her hand. She immediately gestured with her right hand, inviting Yu to sit on the sofa in front of her desk and sat back down in her chair. Still seated, she pulled a design that was leaning against the side of her desk up onto the desk top and pushed it forward so that Yu could see it.

"I showed the samples you brought in the last time you were here to about ten different places, but only one showed any interest in it. It's run by a Guatemalan family that owns a small factory in East Los Angeles. They print textiles for export to Brazil. They said they want big, flashy, brightly colored designs for cotton. Since you didn't have any samples with large designs, they asked me to have you make a different one by enlarging this design. They placed an order, saying they liked the colors in your sample. Here's the telephone number," said Fiona as she pulled a scrap of paper with the name and phone number on it from her drawer and handed it to Yu.

"The factory owner's name is Tony Contrelas. See, it's written here. If you have any questions, please ask him yourself. He says he's in a hurry. Can you get it done within a week?" Fiona rattled off all these questions at lightening speed.

Yu was unsure how to answer. She had just drawn twenty designs and shown them to Fiona in a hit-or-miss fashion, but even so, she was disappointed. Nonetheless, maybe she should be glad to get even one response.

"So, this is a definite order, right? Will they pay the usual amount?"

"Of course they'll pay. I don't know if it will be the usual amount or not. The economy is not good right now. You need to be patient. I'll send the contract to them by the end of the day."

Yu felt frustrated. In those days, everybody was pretending that the economy was bad but then refusing to raise the price for designs. She wasn't sure where Fiona had shown her twenty designs, so there was a chance that they could be pirated by someone. Unlike literature, music, or designs for sophisticated machinery, the ideas and colors used in the visual arts could be knocked-off in no time. Yu therefore decided to take her other samples back home with her.

The young woman who had shown Yu in knocked and then opened the door to announce another visitor.

"Okay. Let him in," said Fiona in a shrill voice.

A blond, cold-looking young man wearing a loose-fitting white shirt and white trousers and canvas sneakers without socks slid smoothly into the room. A small diamond sparkled on his earlobe.

Without even glancing in Yu's direction, he spoke to Fiona in a saccharine voice that didn't jive with his face. "Hi, Fiona. You gave me such wonderful news that I couldn't sit still at home. Marvelous! Marvelous! You are wonderful!" Then he gave her a kiss on each cheek.

"Hello, darling. You are wonderful yourself, *mon petit Jean*," said Fiona, using the French pronunciation of the name. "That design you gave me was another really good piece, so I took it all over to recommend it. There have already been inquiries about it from five places!"

In stark contrast to her emphasis on how hard times were

when she'd been talking to Yu just a few minutes earlier, Fiona was positively joyful when she began speaking to John or whatever his name was.

"I don't care if she calls him '*Jean*' or 'John,' but '*mon petit*' and 'Hello darling'? I certainly never had her greet me like that," thought Yu. "It would make me sick if she did, but still . . ." Yu hastily gathered up the samples she'd gotten back from Fiona and, making a perfunctory farewell, left the office and went out again onto the bustling streets of the Wilshire area. As she unlocked the door of her car, Yu went over Fiona's behavior again in her mind.

This kind of thing happened a lot. In the design biz, unless something was extraordinarily refined, it was often hard to determine if it was good. Moreover, what ordinary people called beautiful was often regarded as such simply because someone important recommended it. In other words, people are easily brainwashed and, swept away by a design agent's palaver, they frequently buy things that are mere fluff.

However, Yu's agent, Fiona, was not promoting Yu's work, and that often hurt her feelings. Having been told that no one expressed any interest, there was nothing more she could say, but . . . She never was able to ask Fiona why she didn't push her work. It might simply be a matter of a mismatch between Fiona's and Yu's taste. Yet it would be hard to find another agent, probably because Yu was Asian and female.

Yu had started to become aware of this subtle discrimination around the time her older daughter Miki had entered elementary school. The students in the school were almost all white, while Miki's cute face displayed a nice mix of East and West.

One day, Miki had come home from school almost in tears, crying, "Mommy, Beth and Lucy were invited to Davy's birthday party but I wasn't!"

Yu had comforted Miki by telling her, "That kind of thing happens, you know. He couldn't invite everyone in the class." Still, though she didn't show it, Yu had been quite upset. Compared to Yu, Miki was not so readily identifiable as Asian, and yet even she . . . She had tried to follow the advice of her other Japanese friends and think of Miki as overly sensitive to such apparent slights, but that was no excuse for it. Something similar had happened at Christmas and left Miki quite miserable.

When the same type of thing happened to her younger daughter, Ann, Yu began to casually observe the situation whenever she went to school to pick up the girls. She noticed that the mothers of the white children were often brusque with Ann but treated other white children in a very friendly manner. She briefly explained the situation to Ann's teacher, who was a white woman, and said that she would like the school to create opportunities to enlighten both the parents and students about racial problems, but the teacher would hear none of it, claiming that many of the parents of the children in the school were well educated so they were not in the least discriminatory.

It was around then that Yu had noticed that the teachers' treatment of her daughters was different from their treatment of white children.

Bob had told her, "No, that's not true. You're being paranoid." He didn't seem to be actually trying to insult Yu, so she wasn't sure if he was simply avoiding the issue by making excuses for white society, or if he really believed what he was saying. In any case, his words didn't bring her any comfort.

She would have felt much better if he had instead said, "It's true—this country is really discriminatory and it's terrible. They're idiots!" and then told her that he would go talk to the teacher himself.

When the girls entered high school and Miki called herself Asian, he had been quite shocked and took a good look at her face. Later, he told Yu, "I was totally caught off guard. I guess I never once thought of them as Asians." At the time, Yu couldn't believe her own husband had said something like that.

What kind of explanation was she supposed to give for the barriers between her daughters and the white children and adults at school? Nothing could be as cruel as passing on the mistakes of parents to their children. When asked why by her young children, Yu falteringly told them that those people were wrong. That's why she had become so sensitive to such inequalities.

Recently, whenever Bob started to say something like "The person in the family who's making the most money should get priority," Yu would immediately launch a counterattack.

"I'm female and I'm Asian, and Japanese at that—the most hated Asians in this country; that means I'm working with two and a half handicaps. Sorry, but don't you think you have a duty to help me out more than spouses in all-white couples? I bet if I were a white male, I'd be getting twice as much for my designs."

"Enough. I've heard that all before."

"That's because you keep saying the same thing, you know. These days, talk like that would get you slapped by a younger woman!"

Yu drove off, leaving the street on which Fiona's office was located and turning onto Wilshire Boulevard, where she realized that she was close to the Bullock's Wilshire department store. She rarely came to this area and figured she should take this opportunity to look at the textile patterns used in the latest dress fashions, so she went into the sturdy Art Deco building.

As she waited in front of the elevator, she imagined that she just might run into a movie star like Marlene Dietrich, wearing a hat with a feather on it, or Lana Turner, or that handsome Cary Grant. Ever since the old days, whenever they shoot a movie scene in a department store, it's always at the Bullock's Wilshire, the classiest department store in Los Angeles. Coming in here suddenly made her feel as if she'd become a movie star herself, making her forget the unpleasant feeling she'd had earlier. "People in India, Mexico, Japan—the world over—looked at America through the movies, just like I do, even after living here all these years," she thought. "Maybe the reason so many immigrants come here is that they are under the illusion that they, too, can lead the luxurious life of a Hollywood star. That's a big mistake, you guys."

3

Yu and her family lived in a suburban community whose sole connection to Los Angeles proper was Sunset Boulevard. The town was situated on the Pacific coast on the westernmost point in the continental United States; behind it lay the Santa Monica Mountains, upon whose foothills the entire town nestled. The family home stood on a cliff overlooking the ocean. You might say that Bob was successful, as they had purchased the house with money he had earned on his own. That success owed a lot to his being a member of the elite class of top earners in American society—white males. Yu sometimes felt guilty about partaking of it.

It was almost twilight. The setting sun had dyed the western sky vermilion. A mist was coming in, enveloping Catalina Island, which had been clearly visible floating on the horizon that morning. The green chaparral and anise, which had completely covered the cliff in front of the house during the winter rains, had taken on a red glow.

Seeing that the light was changing, Yu decided she should stop now so that she didn't make a mistake in the coloring of her design. She laid her open sketchbook down on her desk, on which her ruler, compass, colored pencils, paints, palette and brushes lay scattered. She got up from her chair and raised both hands to stretch. Then, taking her reading glasses in her right hand, she ran her fingers through her graying hair, which was tied up in a bun.

Their yard was home to a variety of plants. In addition to the Satsuma tangerine tree, there were persimmon and navel orange trees that Yu had planted when the family had moved in. During the winter, the translucent yellow of daffodils dotted the entire garden, while the pale purple of lavender colored it all year round, and the dark purple of irises tinged it in early spring. It was delightful, but tough to keep up.

They'd hired a stream of Japanese-American and Mexican gardeners over the years, but these days, none of them used rakes to sweep up the fallen leaves; instead, they used something called a blower, which was powered by a gasoline motor and looked like a large hair dryer. It made a tremendous rumbling noise—enough to wake up anyone sleeping within a kilometer of the house. Even worse, the garden was already dry and dusty, and the blower sent not only the fallen leaves but also the dust from the entire yard up into the air, making it hard to know whether they'd come to clean or just make the air dirty. Whenever they came, Yu would rush around the house closing up the windows.

After they left, any flower seedlings that had been planted the previous day were all dried out by hot air from the blower and lay on the ground, completely wilted. Yu sometimes suspected that the gardeners were in league with the nursery and got a commission for the havoc they wreaked. She had repeatedly asked them not to use the blower, telling them that it wouldn't bother her if a few leaves were left behind—that that was actually more natural—but she had been unable to get through to them.

The upshot was that for about two years, Yu had been doing the gardening work herself. It was just a matter of pulling weeds and gathering fallen leaves with a rake, but when she had tried to get Bob to help, he had claimed that even the simple act of raking leaves might be enough to give him a heart attack, so she'd given up on that idea. At any rate, Bob had grown up in New York and the only tree names he knew were pine and cedar; he was not interested in the garden.

Recently, however, Yu's back had been hurting her, so she had hired the man who was looking after a neighbor's garden, a Mexican named Jose.

Previously, when he'd been doing the neighbor's gardening, Jose had often seen Yu working in her yard all on her own, dressed in a pair of worn-out jeans and always wearing one of Bob's old shirts over her top.

"Are your employers good people?" he'd asked.

Yu had not been able to figure out what he meant by this, so she just looked at his brown face and pondered on his question. After quite some time, she suddenly realized, 'Oh—he thinks I'm the maid!'

Finally, she replied, "I live in this house."

"Are you a widow?" he asked next.

This must have been because in America, gardening is considered men's work, but only Yu was doing it at her house.

"No," answered Yu.

"Japs great. Work real hard," commented Jose.

He seemed to be praising her, but Yu didn't know how to respond. She couldn't very well say "thank you" after having been called a "Jap." Yet it occurred to her that even if she put on a frown and lectured him, telling him that it wasn't nice to call people that, it may be that this was the only way of referring to Japanese people that he knew and that he had meant no harm, so she ended up saying nothing at all.

After that, Yu began trying to make Bob feel guilty, frequently telling him, "The neighbor's gardener asked me if I'm the maid or a widow. That's because gardening is considered men's work in this country, you know. Don't you think that makes the man of the house look pretty bad?"

Before she had hired Jose, the situation had seemed hopeless. The garden had been literally buried in leaves from the large eucalyptus tree, which seemed to rain down all summer. The leaves contain an oil that stops plants from growing, so they couldn't be left on top of the flower beds for long. Yu envied the neighbor, whose garden always looked neat as a pin.

However, when she'd started to observe the situation more closely, it seemed to her that after Jose left the neighbor's yard, there were more leaves in her garden. Since there wasn't a wall between the two properties, the blower was blasting the leaves over here. That was when Yu realized that the best way to get rid of this problem was for her to hire the gardener, too. Yet because she insisted that he not use the blower, she ended up paying almost double the amount he charged her neighbor.

A sturdy barrel of a man with bronze-colored skin, Jose was about forty years old. He could speak English a bit, albeit haltingly. It turned out, however, that he was very macho. He boasted in his heavily accented English, "Missus, I got eight children."

Yu did not know how to respond, so she just said, "Oh." She still had no idea whether he had been bragging because, as a devout Catholic, he'd followed the Pope's orders and had his wife bear eight children, or if he had been putting his machismo on display, or suggesting that he needed more money because his living expenses were high, or perhaps even, judging from the fact that Yu was Japanese and the stereotype of people from her country was that they were rich, asking her to pay a lot. Yu had wanted to tell him that he was barking up the wrong tree.

Since keeping up the yard was such a burden, Yu had been suggesting that they move to a condo, but Bob showed no signs of a willingness to move. One reason was probably that Bob had a work room in this house in addition to his office downtown. Yu had her studio here, too, and neither one of them wanted to move their materials for work from the places they were used to using them in.

In addition, house prices in the area had dropped by a third in recent years. The economy of Southern California owed its prosperity to the munitions industry, so the recent moves towards disarmament, coupled with the general economic malaise the entire country was experiencing, meant that it was in worse shape than other areas.

"Remember when those people wanted to buy this house three years ago—when prices were at their peak?" asked Bob. "If we'd sold it then, we'd be financially set right now. You were against it so we didn't go through with it," he complained.

"If you wanted to sell it, you should have looked into it. You didn't act on your idea, did you? And if we'd bought a condo then, the price for that would have been at its peak, too, so we wouldn't have been any better off anyway. I suppose if we could have kept the cash, that might have been great, but we need a place to live, don't we. Don't put all the blame on me!"

Yu was recalling this conversation when she glanced at the clock on the table. It was past six. Time for the news. She left her studio and went to the family room, where she turned on the television.

4

The screen showed an urban street corner. Everything looked beige. A long truck loaded with sand and gravel had broken down right in the middle of a wide intersection. On the asphalt next to the truck, a large white man in blue jeans and a white T-shirt was lying, blood dripping from his head like a steer that had been slaughtered. Two or three black men were moving back and forth nearby, and then one of them threw what looked like a brick at the man on the ground, who appeared to be already dead. The man who had thrown it then lifted one leg in a dancing motion and walked away.

Yu was stunned by the savagery of this act and kept her eyes glued to the screen as she lowered herself onto the sofa in front of the TV. She couldn't make any sense out of what she was seeing. What city could this be? Somewhere in the Republic of South Africa? The people's clothes seemed to be too nice for that, and the people themselves too well-fed. Eventually, the sound of a helicopter became audible, and then the shrill voice of a male reporter could be heard saying, "This is the corner of Normandie and Florence in the South Central area."

Yu made a first with her right hand and brought it to her mouth and leaned forward and continued to stare at the TV.

Now she saw a brown van stop in the upper left hand corner of the screen. A group of black men went over and began dragging a man from the car. A group of three or more black men went over to it and immediately could be seen dragging a man from the car. He appeared to be Asian. Blood was dripping from his face. Toward the front of the screen, a car got stopped and a Latino woman was pulled out. She was injured, too. It was like wild animals had been let loose to do as much violence as they pleased. It was all too cruel, and yet the police were nowhere to be seen.

Now that she thought about it, wasn't it this morning that Bob had said, "Today is the day that they're going to rule on the Rodney King case." Yu hadn't had the news on, so she had no idea what the verdict had been.

She had, however, read about the incident in the paper and seen television programs about it on a number of occasions. It had taken place in March 1991, in Los Angeles. A black man, Rodney King, had been caught for speeding and for some reason or other (the police said afterward that he would not do what they told him to), four policemen ganged up on him and beat him so badly that his face was swollen beyond all recognition. Even before that, it had been widely known that the treatment of minorities by the white police in the city was cruel and insensitive, but it was rare for there to actually be a formal complaint about it because the police would suppress evidence. Nonetheless, there had been frequent rumors in the black community about this kind of thing.

This time, however, the brutality had been captured in toto on videotape. A white man who lived in the neighborhood had just purchased a camcorder and happened to be trying it out when the incident took place right in front of his eyes. At the time, he probably never dreamed that his videotape would end up being shown all over the world. However, he did take the tape to a television station, and that's why the incident became such a big deal. All the TV stations had picked it up and aired it.

In recent years, the number of people from minority groups living in the region had soared, and minorities now accounted for more than half of the population of Los Angeles. They condemned this act of police brutality, and the public outrage was so strong that the perpetrators were put on trial. Yet even though the mayor at the time was a black man, Tom Bradley, power still remained in the hands of the whites.

The state Court of Appeals had replaced the initial judge for the proceedings and granted a change of venue motion, agreeing that the media coverage in Los Angeles County had been too intense and there was a danger of the trial causing political unrest. However, the real reason that the trial was moved to another county was that if it had been held in downtown Los Angeles, a large number of blacks would have attended the sessions, and the authorities didn't want a disturbance each time testimony was given.

Also, a jury in Los Angeles was likely to be more than half black. This would have been disadvantageous to the white police officers. That was one of the reasons why the white judge changed the venue to the all-white community of Simi Valley in neighboring Ventura County. Since the jury was selected from residents of that area, it was a given that there would not be a single black person chosen to serve on it. The panel of twelve was split evenly among Republicans and Democrats and included a banker, a realtor, a nurse, a housewife, a park keeper and a mental health practitioner. They had been selected so as to be disadvantageous to blacks, with the only minorities on the jury being one Latino and one Asian. There had never been any question about what the result would be.

The TV announced that the white policemen had been acquitted. The screen still showed a bird's-eye view of the city. The police were nowhere in sight. The blacks gathered at the intersection could be seen swarming like ants into a liquor store on the corner. When at last they came out, they were all carrying paper bags filled with six-packs of beer, bottles of whiskey, and potato chips. Around the time that the store appeared to have been completely ransacked, smoke started coming out from the rear of the building, and eventually, the shop was engulfed in flames. Yu wondered what in the world had happened to the storeowner and the clerks who'd been on duty—were they still alive?

Because of the noise from the helicopter, the reporter's voice was unclear and sometimes was drowned out entirely. Yu figured that they probably couldn't have filmed on the ground. If they'd sent a white cameraman into this enraged mob, he would have been beaten up instantly, but they probably didn't have many black cameramen in their employ.

The camera on the helicopter panned over to the corner of the intersection diagonally opposite the liquor store, where a gasoline station stood. It was nothing but gas pumps and a small, hut-like building in the center of a square, cement-covered lot, so it looked like there was nothing there that could be stolen, but nonetheless, people were going in and out of the small shop. The concrete was littered with trash. Yu couldn't imagine what they were walking away with. She was just happy to see that they hadn't set the pumps on fire.

A long-distance shot showed a large number of people swarming in and out of a liquor store about a block away. Eventually, this shop was also enveloped in flames. It had been set upon in the same way as the first liquor store. Yu wondered if this had been planned in advance. How outrageous! But in any case, it seemed strange that no fire engines had come to deal with the blazes.

Yu suddenly recalled something Bob had said a week earlier: "I wonder when they're going to reach a verdict. If the police are cleared, there might be rioting."

"Oh my goodness—this is a riot!" she thought. Frightened, she tightly grabbed hold of both of her arms, which were covered in goose bumps. "This is the suburbs, so we're not right there, but what in the world is going to happen? The people being attacked at that intersection are not just whites, but Asians and Latinos, too."

Her thoughts raced on. "Where did Bob say he was going today? He doesn't have any clients in that area, so he couldn't possibly be driving through there now, could he?"

She had thought that rioting was something that happened in places like South Africa, Haiti or Panama. It had never occurred to her that a riot might break out in the town where she lived. She was really glad that she'd gone into town to see Fiona two days ago and not today.

What would happen if the rioting reached here?

When she'd first arrived in California twenty years earlier, Yu felt like she'd come to paradise. Once the rains of winter are gone, the skies of southern California are immediately bathed in radiant sunlight and turn a glorious transparent blue—in stark contrast to dreary New York, with its frequent rain and snow. Now it appeared that she'd been under a temporary delusion that this meant there was "tranquility" here. When they'd moved to this city in 1970, you couldn't tell that the Watts Riots had occurred here only five years earlier.

But then she recalled one of Bob's friends jokingly recounting his experience in those riots. "It was really hot that summer, you see, so I set off for Crenshaw Boulevard to buy an air conditioner, and as I was driving along the Santa Monica Freeway, bullets came whistling by me, phew, phew, from both sides," he'd said animatedly, turning his head first to the right and then to the left and using the index finger of each hand to illustrate how the bullets had come whizzing by. "I wondered what was happening, and when I came down off the freeway, there was a riot going on! When I got to the appliance store, the place was on fire!"

Yu thought back to the Los Angeles of twenty years ago. "When we moved here from New York—that must have been the calm after things had more or less settled down. The city had seemed like the embodiment of peace, it was so relaxed . . ." Then she reconsidered this view. "No," she thought, "the first couple of years after we moved here the kids were so little that we must have been just too tied up with our own concerns to even notice anything."

The people Bob associated with were all wealthy and lived on the West Side of Los Angeles—places like Beverly Hills, Brentwood and Santa Monica, so probably the only people they talked to were upper middle-class whites. Still, it had seemed like the people of Los Angeles were waking up a little when they had replaced the white mayor, Sam Yorty, with the black Tom Bradley.

At any rate, there was plenty of money flowing in this area thanks to the munitions and movie industries, so even if minority groups weren't making anywhere near as much as the people profiting from those industries, there were still plenty of jobs for them, and that may have been why things had been quiet here. The Vietnam War, which lasted fourteen years, had had a huge impact on American society. Even though industries that supported the military had prospered, those related to civilian needs had been neglected, so people had no choice but to rely on imports. That's why the economy in areas of the country that had no military equipment manufacturers was so bad. After the war in Vietnam ended, the Republican Party stayed in power for another decade, and during that time, it cut taxes for the rich and increased the taxes on the lower and middle classes.

The people in show business were so arrogant—living in palatial mansions, going to power breakfasts and power lunches at the Beverly Hills Hotel, the Hotel Bel Air or expensive restaurants like Spago, driving around in their Mercedes, Porsches, BMWs and Jaguars, and shamelessly partying at night, accompanied by beautiful women decked out in diamonds and sapphires and parading around in outfits from Armani, Versace, Chanel and Lacroix. When the poor saw these show-offs on the street or on television, or were hired to care for their children or clean their homes, they could not help but see the contrast between such extravagant lifestyles and their own situation, where they could work their entire lives and never get ahead. It was like the difference between heaven and earth. Hit by this realization, they had no way to vent their resentment, and their despair was transformed into anger.

Then the Soviet Union had collapsed and the Berlin Wall had crumbled, meaning there was even less demand for military equipment. Of course, it was Southern California that was the hardest hit by this development. Thousands of people lost their jobs. On top of that, virtually all of the manufacturers who had plants in the city relocated to places like Mexico, Southeast Asia and China, where labor was cheaper. This meant greater profits for the investors, but the first ones to lose their jobs were the minorities working at those plants. And African-Americans suffered the most. They were the ones who were most discriminated against, so they were the first ones to lose their jobs.

Although Exxon Oil made 8.2 billion dollars, it was exempt from paying federal income taxes, and corporate giants like City Bank, Campbell Soup, and Gallo Wine were all receiving government subsidies—that is, welfare—which totaled billions of dollars. Nevertheless, the government began trying to cut the $300 monthly welfare payments to single mothers and started trimming education expenses as well as funds for public facilities and other support for the poor. The number of homeless people in the area rapidly ballooned. If only they had diverted the welfare given to corporations and used it to educate the children in the poorer areas, the kids would have been able to learn higher level technical skills . . .

The income of the wealthiest five percent of the population accounted for half of the earnings in the entire country. To make up for the deficits incurred during the Savings and Loan scandal, in which President H. W. Bush's son Neil was involved, the federal government had spent the equivalent of $2,000 per person in tax money. Yet the Bronx and Harlem still had not been rebuilt after the New York riots of 1977; weeds towered where buildings had once stood. The poor began to see their situation as hopeless. There was no way they could pull themselves up without the help of the government or big business.

The collapse of Communism meant that there was no longer any organized competition for capitalism, so Americans, without a viable enemy in the world, felt free to unabashedly show their greed without worrying about their reputation. The poor were abandoned, and money became all that mattered in every aspect of life.

Seeing this transformation in moral standards, Yu felt that the real enemy of America—which operated on the pretense that it was a free country built on free enterprise—was not

Communism, but capitalism.

Yu could still remember how she had heard the Reverend King's "I have a dream" speech on the radio shortly after she'd come to America; his words and voice had had such an impact on her that she had made his dream her own. At that time, she had learned that it is people who discriminate against others because of the color of their skin or because of their disabilities who are wrong, and that the people who are discriminated against are not to blame. Were those words nothing more than an echo? In moving from Martin Luther King to Rodney King, had Americans lost their dream? Yu sometimes wondered if both North and South America were fated to reach this state.

Since American industries no longer served consumers, Japan had taken over that task and was making big money at it, so it came under increasingly harsh criticism. The American government made the yellow people of Japan scapegoats for this failure in its policy, and "Japan bashing" began.

It was during this period that the Gulf War took place. It was a typical capitalist war. One Arab state invaded another and then President Bush suddenly turned Saddam Hussein into a villain and declared war on Iraq, even though only a year earlier, Iraq had been hailed as a friendly nation and given large amounts of weapons and money. The real reason for the war could be surmised by anyone who could read the newspapers: it was intended to prop up the ailing munitions and oil industries and thereby help the economy recover. The results of this government scheme did not follow the conventional principles of capitalism, however, and the economy went from bad to worse.

For the past two or three years, every time Yu had gone downtown, she had felt that it was just a matter of time until something happened. She had not been sure how it would come about, but now that it had, she was bracing for the worst. How long would it continue and how far would the flames reach?

The rage that blacks felt about the government's unfairness had been transformed into fire and smoke. Yu could understand their anger. But how could she possibly convey to people who were in such a fury that she understood them a little? Before they killed her? The mob she was facing on her TV screen did not seem to care at all about what the people they were beating up were thinking. In fact, the people they were pummeling might even be on their side.

Yu was transfixed by the television. Before she knew it, it was seven o'clock. She needed to get something ready for dinner. Yet her entire body was trembling. The sight of Asian Americans and Latinos being beaten up petrified her. She had always thought that blacks regarded Asian Americans and Latinos as their allies, since they, too, were minorities. Perplexed, she went into the kitchen, where the setting sun could be seen through the half-open mini blinds. There, she opened the door of the refrigerator, which was taller than she was. She found a little chicken, some tofu, and a few scallions, tomatoes and cucumbers—just enough to eke out a dinner for two.

Then suddenly, Yu was struck by a thought: "Our family wouldn't be safe no matter which group of people was being beaten up. *Homma ni!*—I mean, really!" She hadn't really thought much about Bob's race since they'd gotten married, and certainly she'd never been forced to be as aware of it as she had been today. It dawned on her that no matter what your race, you weren't safe in this country. This was gradually becoming true all over the world, but still . . .

The world was one big contradiction. On the one hand,

borders between countries were being broken down as products were being shipped all over the globe, but at the same time, within the cities of a single nation, different ethnic groups—no, sometimes even people from the same ethnic group—were splitting up according to the degree of color in their skin and glaring at each other. What the world needs is for everyone to become colorblind, Yu thought.

She phoned Bob's office, but couldn't get through. Had someone taken out the telephone company or perhaps cut the lines? This was the kind of time when phones were needed most . . . Yu became extremely uneasy. Where was Bob? She thought he was at his office in Santa Monica, but couldn't be sure. She hoped that he'd make it home safely.

She was grateful that their two daughters were not in the country. When she had asked them to give up on their plans to study abroad because it was so expensive, they had both completely ignored what she'd said, just like they always did. At the time, she'd been unhappy with them, but now she was glad they'd gone. Tokyo and Rome were probably safe now. Actually, everywhere outside of Japan is probably dangerous, she thought. In Rome, you never know when a terrorist start shooting. All the same, right now Rome was probably safer than Hollywood, the place many young people in this area chose to live.

Yu's elder daughter Miki looked more Asian than Caucasian. She had a head of black hair, and although her nose was bigger than many Japanese, her eyes were black and not as big as Bob's, and she was only a little taller than Yu. She had majored in Eastern art history at Tufts University in Boston, but for some reason she had gone off to Japan to do research on costumes used in Japanese Noh drama and had been living there for three years now. Who knows how she thought she could make a living in the future. Bob was still sending her money to cover her living expenses, but prices in Tokyo were exorbitant and her budget so tight that she'd started teaching English at a trading company to make ends meet.

Even there she encountered discrimination based on skin color. During a telephone conversation, she had complained, "As long as someone has blond hair and blue eyes, Japanese people think they can speak English really well—even if they're a complete airhead! So they get paid more than I do. It's unbelievable!"

When she heard that, Yu angrily thought, "Things are the same everywhere." All the same, she sighed as she wondered how old Miki would be before they could finally stop sending her money.

Their outgoing younger daughter, Ann, was also a problem. She had taken Italian at Barnard College in New York and gone to Rome on a junior year abroad program. No sooner had she arrived there than she had a boyfriend and started saying that she was not coming back home. Unlike Miki, Ann's face resembled Bob's, but her hair was black (the gene for black hair must be particularly strong), so her face could easily be taken for an Italian's. She was also very tall. Yu had often joked that her DNA had been completely lost in Ann. But the real question was, what did she want to do with her life? Needless to say, Bob was paying for all of her school and living expenses. And prices in Italy were steep, too.

There was the sound of a key in the back door. It rattled for a long time. It must be Bob. It was taking him longer to get it in the keyhole these days—perhaps another sign of age? Yu was relieved at the sight of Bob's face when he finally came through the door. Yet in the light of the entranceway lamp, his face seemed sad and the number of wrinkles in it appeared to have increased in the course of the day. Bob also must have felt relieved to find Yu safe and sound; he embraced her without even stopping to put down the briefcase he had in his hand.

"The phones were cut off. I was so worried," Yu cried. "I didn't really think you would have gone to the area around Florence and Normandie, but even so, the way things are going, who knows what'll happen and how far it'll spread? Especially since the police are nowhere in sight. There are fires raging all over and the fire engines aren't coming to put them out. Everything's just being left to burn. I was so worried!" Even now, her body was frozen with fear.

"It's just awful," Bob said, blinking his olive-colored eyes and hugging his black leather briefcase with his papers from work in it. "If it goes on like this for a week, there will be war on the streets of Los Angeles, and the whole city will be destroyed. I hear that the reason the fire engines aren't coming is because the police aren't there, so it's too dangerous to take them out. The rioters might go after the firemen. You can get more up-to-date news on the car radio than you can on TV. Did you hear that Koreatown has been attacked?"

"What?" Yu was very surprised to hear that. It was not all that far from the expansive neighborhood known as Koreatown to Little Tokyo. She was not so provincial as to be relieved that it was not Little Tokyo that was under attack, but she was half surprised at herself, a member of a minority group, being so out of touch with the psychology of minorities that she had not expected attacks on other minorities.

"Why? Why? Why Koreatown?"

The number of immigrants from Korea had risen dramatically during the past twenty years. They were the third largest group of Asian immigrants in Los Angeles after Filipinos and

Chinese—far outnumbering the Japanese. Traditionally, the number of Asians entering the country had been restricted, so it had been much smaller than the number of Europeans coming, but in 1965, President Johnson expanded the quota for Asian immigrants and their numbers rose rapidly.

Of course, if there is a war in another country, many people will leave that country as refugees, and if the U.S. is involved in that war, it's reasonable for America to accept refugees from that nation. Still, this policy resulted in a massive influx of immigrants, with large numbers coming from Asia alone, starting with orphans and war brides from the Korean War, and then later, refugees from Vietnam, Cambodia and other parts of Asia. Some people said that because South Korea had sent soldiers to fight in the Vietnam War, Korean immigrants had been given priority.

During the 1960s and '70s, Japan was experiencing an economic upturn, and there were plenty of jobs in Japan, so there was no need to emigrate. In contrast, Korea was still a poor country, so many Koreans came to the States for economic reasons. In addition, Korea was under a military regime during the seventies, so many intellectuals left out of frustration, while students who had come to America to study often stayed on to avoid the draft. Those immigrants then brought over their families.

Since the Korean War had been fought in their own country, the Korean immigrants could not forget the privations they suffered there. Moreover, the Korean Peninsula was still divided and the government was very unstable, so it was said that many Koreans didn't want to go back to their country.

More recently, however, Korea had become an affluent nation, and many Korean immigrants were engineers, doctors and other highly educated people. However, because they couldn't speak English, they couldn't get jobs in their own professions right away. Some brought along a little in savings and came looking for businesses they could run privately, while those who hadn't brought a nest egg often borrowed from Korean mutual financing associations. They would buy up the rights to the liquor stores which had been rapidly increasing in areas where blacks lived, or become painters or pool cleaners. However, they couldn't afford expensive buildings, so inevitably, many Korean immigrants wound up setting up businesses and living in the area where the riots were now going on. These people had worked so hard and built such fine neighborhoods, but now . . .

Was all that stuff they wrote in the newspapers—about how this city was doing well as a "melting pot" or a "salad bowl" of all different kinds of people mixed together—nothing more than wishful thinking?

Yu had been thinking that something was going to happen, but she had thought it would be way off in a city in the east or the south. However, just because of the Rodney King incident, it was *her* town that had been set aflame.

James Baldwin, a man who had experienced terrible discrimination, had clearly taught her what the extremes of discrimination were like; now, the title of his book—*The Fire Next Time*—was coming to life right in front of her eyes.

"Who's attacking Koreatown? Those rioters?"

"That's right. For now, at least, the rioters are blacks, and most of the liquor store owners are Korean. And there's a liquor store on almost every corner in the black neighborhoods. The owners are making a profit off black people. Also, remember a while back, when a Korean woman storeowner decided that a young black girl had robbed her, so she shot the girl with a pistol? She got a suspended sentence, right? Blacks are saying the sentencing was unfair and are taking their anger out on Koreans. Of course, they're even madder at whites, but it just so happens that it's the Koreans who live close to the black neighborhoods, so they're within easier reach," Bob explained.

"Oh. So who was attacked during the Watts Riots in '65?"

"The people living nearby at that time were Jewish, so they were the targets then. They got scared after that and moved away."

"New immigrants don't have much money so they end up living in dangerous neighborhoods. That's the history of immigration," thought Yu.

Like Tokyo, Los Angeles is very spread out, and the people who live in the areas where housing is expensive, like Beverly Hills and Brentwood, or Santa Monica and Pacific Palisades along the coast, were almost all white. In the rest of the metropolitan area, there were some neighborhoods separated by group—Latino, white, Asian, black—and others where the groups were all thrown together and in fierce competition with each other. The South Central area where the rioting was going on was mainly black, but some Latinos lived there too, and Koreatown bordered it on the north. By car, it was about five minutes west of the downtown area, where Little Tokyo, City Hall, and Police Headquarters were situated. Next to Koreatown on the west lay Hollywood. In any case, because minorities make up sixty percent of the population of Los Angeles, they're all intermingled.

The Crenshaw area, which was now under attack, was the home of a lot of Japanese a couple of decades ago. The fishmonger who used to come to Yu's house had lived there. The area had also housed Japanese movie theaters such as the Kabuki and the Kokusai, which was part of the Shochiku theater chain. Yu had often gone there to see movies. These days, many of the

Japanese residents had become rich and moved to the west side and to the suburbs, so there were a lot fewer living in the old neighborhood, but the elderly and those unable to move were undoubtedly still living there.

"I have no idea which side I should be on," thought Yu. "I hate unfairness too, you know. The degree may be quite different, but I also experience discrimination all the time in my line of work. Still—the way they're taking the white police and the Korean woman who killed the black girl and won unfair court settlements and lumping them together with the white driver and the Korean shop owners who are being assaulted now, plus the many different Asian populations—from Cambodia, Vietnam, the Philippines, China, Japan and Korea . . .

"The people who are protesting against discrimination are themselves guilty of discriminating. How is this to be interpreted? Even if you're burdened by a long history of discrimination, the ancestors of the people under attack here now may have had nothing to do with that. The forebears of the Koreans you're beating up may well be the children of people who suffered cruelty at the hands of the Japanese when they colonized Korea during the militaristic prewar era."

It was then that it dawned on Yu that the victims of the riots were people with really bad luck, who just happened to be in the wrong place at the wrong time. Take, for example, that white driver: He just happened to come to the intersection of Florence and Normandie at that particular time. If he had skipped lunch and gone through there an hour earlier, he would have gotten through without the slightest problem.

The rioters, judging from appearances, did not seem to have any special political convictions. From what she could see on television, these young men had simply seized the chance to act up and were doing it just for kicks. Why, the young guy who had thrown the brick or whatever at the dump truck driver seemed to be doing something like a dance afterward!

It all seemed to be a matter of timing. Six years earlier, Japanese Prime Minister Yasuhiro Nakasone had said that the level of intelligence of blacks and Mexicans was low. If he had said that recently, Little Tokyo would have been burned to the ground—that's how fierce "Japan bashing" had become.

The eleven o'clock news showed a melee in front of City Hall and Police Headquarters, as well as stores being looted here and there, and others being burned down. The police appeared to have finally come out, but it seemed they were just too late. The looting went on well after dark. Now it was not just blacks, but a large number of Latinos as well. The announcer reported that by late evening, there were fires burning at one hundred and fifty locations and gunshots from shootouts could be heard.

No one said anything about where Police Chief Daryl Gates was. This was the guy who was rumored to be at odds with Mayor Tom Bradley, and who the Christopher Commission—which had investigated the complaint of police brutality in the Rodney King incident—had recommended should resign, but had refused to do so. It seemed like the riots served as an example of how things could blow up when the mayor and police chief of a city didn't get along.

But Yu couldn't just sit here fascinated by it all. Even though her home was a thirty-minute freeway ride away from the intersection where the riots had started, the incessant wail of sirens could still be heard. According to the TV, the looting and burning were spreading westward—toward the area where Yu lived.

5

April 30

Yu had been awake all night worrying, but at last it was morning
and she was buried in the newspaper as she ate her breakfast.
The headline on the front page of the *Los Angeles Times* read:

```
All 4 in King Beating Acquitted
Violence Follows Verdicts
Guard Called Out
```

Another headline reported:

```
Rioters Set Fires, Loot Stores; 4 Reported
Dead
Rampage: 106 are wounded or injured and
more than 150 blazes are ignited.
```

The second story included the following details:

```
Rioters . . . stormed police headquarters
and trashed numerous downtown buildings.
Sporadic gunfire flared in the streets.
```

When Yu raised her eyes from the newspaper, she could see

shots of the city going up in flames on the television in the dining room. It didn't look like things were calming down at all—in fact, the violence appeared to be spreading.

Yu turned the page of the newspaper. There she saw a photo of the bloodstained Asian man she'd seen on TV the night before; another picture showed him getting beaten by a black rioter. She was shocked that someone had been taking pictures. The newspaper reported that a brown Jeep Wrangler had been hit by a rock coming straight at the front of the car, breaking the glass in the window. When the car stopped, the Asian man had gotten out of it. A rioter had then hit the man's face with a bottle. The man appeared to be about forty, and Yu wondered if he was Japanese. She'd been living here for decades now, but even so, whenever she saw a picture of an Asian person, the first thing she thought was always, "I wonder if s/he's Japanese."

How terrible, she thought. Today, all Asians are taken for Koreans. To people of other races, we all look alike. Sometimes we're seen as Chinese, sometimes as Japanese. Remember Vincent Chin, that Chinese American who was murdered in the Detroit area because his attackers thought he was Japanese? People don't bother to ask us what our nationality is; they just go ahead and see us as whichever Asian nationality is in the news at the time. That's what happens to the Japanese when they step outside of Japan.

Yu thought back to the time of the border war between China and India—she couldn't quite remember the exact year, but it must have been about thirty years earlier—when she had been standing in front of the Elephanta Caves on an island near Bombay and a group of elementary school students had mistaken her for Chinese and begun throwing stones at her.

Fortunately, they didn't hit her, but it had been terrifying. If

Bob hadn't been white and come out and yelled at them, they wouldn't have stopped. Seeing the two of them together, they may well have been taken aback. Or maybe there were still some vestiges of the British colonial era mentality remaining in those Indian grade-schoolers—a fear of whites. It was thanks to that strange kind of reverse discrimination that she had escaped with her life!

"Bob seems to think I owe him a lot for that," she thought, "but it wasn't Bob's strength that made those school children afraid. It was just the color of his skin." Now he's put on weight, but at that time, he had a hyperactive thyroid and was very skinny. In any case, she couldn't remember the Buddhas in those caves at all. The only thing she could remember was standing on a little hill in front of the caves and looking down at that pack of school kids, all glaring at her intensely!

Then there was the time, two or three years after she'd come to America, when she was out in the New Hampshire countryside and a laborer called her a "Jap." At least that guy hadn't mistaken her nationality. Bob got into an argument with the guy, and Yu had become frightened, so she insisted, "It's okay. People can call me that if they want."

"Idiot!" Bob bellowed. "Don't you know he's insulting you?"

Ever since then, she had gradually become more sensitive to the implications of words and the meanings of various intonations. "It takes a long time to really understand the nuances of a language. But if you don't understand them, you won't see danger when it comes your way," thought Yu.

Through experiences like these, Yu had gradually started to consider the attitude ordinary Japanese have toward Korean and Chinese residents of Japan, as well as toward members of the former outcast group known as *burakumin,* who still experience discrimination in Japanese society today. She realized that because she was part of the majority in Japan, she had never noticed how minority groups in her own country were treated. Even after the war, many Japanese openly displayed their contempt for people from those groups, and there weren't even any laws to protect minorities living in Japan. It was only after she had begun living in America that it dawned on her that in that setting, and even more so under the militaristic conditions prevalent during the war, those people's very lives were at risk—that they were in fact living under conditions very similar to those James Baldwin wrote about.

Yu was startled when the phone rang, as she had thought that the lines were down. It was Meg, her tall and skinny neighbor. She was the kind of person who in Japan would have been nicknamed *"hosokyoku"*—the broadcaster. Meg was in her late thirties, and since she was so good at gathering information, Yu had always thought it strange that she did not have a job.

"Yu-hoo-hoo," she began in her cheery soprano voice, as if she were singing a song. In her mind, the sound "hoo" must have gone with the sound of the name "Yu." "Have you been to the supermarket already?"

"No. Not yet. What's up?"

"It's packed. Everyone's freaking out. They think that with things so bad in the city, trucks won't be able to get this far. So there's a run on the supermarket. First of all, no one knows where the supermarket warehouses are, do they? Maybe they'll be burned down. Then the stores would run out of food. And who knows how long the rioting will go on."

"You're right! We need to go get some food, too," Yu agreed. But she was just saying that. When she heard Meg say, "Who knows how long the rioting will go on," she began trembling and had a hard time talking for a while.

"Do you know where the chief of police was last night?" Meg said nonchalantly, not a trace of fear in her voice.

"No-o-o. Where was he?" Yu's voice cracked as she forced herself to speak.

"You won't believe it. He was on the Westside. Apparently, he was at a Republican fund-raising party not far from here. And he *knew* that there were riots going on! What's more, he ordered police near Florence and Normandie to pull out of the area! That's why everything snowballed. He doesn't get along with the mayor, so he may have been trying to sabotage him." Meg's words came out in a fast and furious torrent. Yu wondered if being tall made you less afraid of things.

"Well, the way things were going yesterday, the police almost certainly would have been targeted, so maybe he wanted to keep them out of harm's way. Weren't John and Bruce afraid when they saw the riots on TV?" Yu asked.

Meg had two sons, one in seventh grade and the other in fifth. Miki and Ann had often been asked to babysit the boys when they were little, so they had frequently been over to her house. Meg and Yu had known each other since then.

"Afraid? No way! They said this was nothing—they've seen much worse stuff in the movies and on TV a bunch of times. They're so used to seeing cruelty on TV that they're completely inured to it."

Hearing that gave Yu goose bumps. What was the world coming to? Were movies and television making people numb to brutality so that weapons manufacturers could make bigger profits? Would mass murder become an everyday occurrence?

After hanging up, Yu went and found Bob in the bathroom, still shaving, and asked him to go buy a week's supply of groceries sometime that day, adding that she didn't really care what he picked up.

"Wouldn't it be better if you went?"

Of course it would. She knew that. But it was hard for her to say that she was too afraid to go.

"Errrr—Koreans are getting beat up in these riots, you know. And I look like a Korean. To the rioters, Japanese and Koreans are one and the same. If you've got an Asian face, you're going to get attacked. And besides, I'm short and not very strong."

"Well, I'm not exactly safe either, you know. That truck driver was white!"

"Well, at least you're bigger than me!"

In the end, Bob went. He liked exchanging information with the neighbors at the supermarket. On his way out the door, Yu called after him, "Anything we can eat will do, so just be sure to buy a lot."

The phone rang. It was their elder daughter Miki calling from Tokyo.

"Mommy! It's awful, isn't it? I saw it on TV. Are things okay where you are? Are both of you all right?"

"Yeah, we're all right. For now, anyway. It's scary, though."

"Yeah—Koreans and Japanese look the same. If you feel afraid, you get out of there, you hear? And if you go somewhere else to be safe, call me as soon as you get there to let me know where you are. Didn't you have a friend in Santa Barbara? You should be safe there. I'm going to call Ann in Rome and let her know that you guys are all right, so you don't have to call her. You be sure to be really careful. Get out of there. I'm so worried about you! I love you, Mommy. Tell Daddy that, too."

Miki was not at all like her sister Ann; although she was a

nervous-type, she was very Japanese in the way she found it difficult to express her emotions—just like Yu. She had never before clearly said, "I love you, Mommy," and the trembling voice with which she said it kept ringing in Yu's ear. It was as if she thought this might be her last chance to say it.

An hour later, Yu heard the garage door open. She was still sitting in front of the television. Shortly afterward, she saw Bob, who'd put on weight recently, through the window. He was coming in through the back yard, two white plastic shopping bags in each hand—so laden down that it looked like he might drop them. Surprised, Yu scurried over to the back door to help him. Opening the door, she scolded him,

"Why didn't you say something to me first? It's too much for your heart to be carrying such a heavy load."

"I didn't want to have to make two trips," he huffed, his pot belly heaving as he gasped for breath.

Yu shook her head at how, ever since he'd been young, Bob had had the habit of rushing through things at odd times but dawdling when haste was really needed.

"Thank you for going shopping," she said. "That's a big help. Miki called just a few minutes ago. She's really worried about us. She actually said, 'I love you,' and told me to tell you that, too."

"Oh? She must be really worried if she said that. I wish I could've talked to her." Bob stopped still in his tracks, the shopping bags in tow. Seeing that he hadn't yet put them down, Yu took the bags from him one at a time and placed them on the floor.

"I ran into Hank at the market," Bob reported, mentioning the name of a neighbor who worked at a newspaper. "He said he's supposed to work the night shift today, but he has no idea how to get downtown."

"On a day like today, will anybody be going to work?"

"Most people won't, but journalists have to."

"I suppose so."

"Do you know where the police chief was?"

"Yeah, Meg told me." This place was like a small town, Yu thought. Meg had undoubtedly heard the news from Hank's wife.

"Beverly Hills wasn't touched. Apparently, the police made sure to protect it by closing off all the roads leading to Beverly Hills—and only those roads. They were trying to protect the rich. It was like they were showing the world that the police exist just for the wealthy."

That's why the minorities always end up doing battle with each other. Rioters always burn down their own neighborhoods, punishing no one but themselves. They'd already burned down supermarkets, clothing stores and other shops that sell the necessities of daily life. Many of them don't have a car—where will they get food? Other than a very few, most of them don't know who created the conditions that have forced them to live such miserable lives. Were they unaware of the old eastern WASP establishment that pulls the government's strings from behind the scenes? Or did the police and military form such a strong wall around the blue bloods that the rioters couldn't get through? No matter where there were riots or any other kind of protest, the eastern establishment in places like Beverly Hills always remained untouched.

6

That night, the eleven o'clock news featured video footage taken from a helicopter; it was clear not only that the city was still burning, but that the arsonists were continuing their march to the west. The fires rose in the sky like the pillars of flame that had lit up the oil fields of Kuwait during the Gulf War. There went another one! Billions of sparks went flying in all directions. The red glow of the raging fires dotted the black of the night sky.

Seeing that, Yu wondered what would have happened if those hot winds that come in from the desert—the Santa Anas—had been blowing today, and shivered at the thought. The fires would have swept through the area along with the strong gusts of dry air, burning up everything from the downtown area through Hollywood, Beverly Hills and Westwood, all the way down to the Santa Monica pier. Indeed, the sole comfort to be found in the situation was that there was no wind.

The daytime shootouts in Koreatown took on the look of a full-blown war. The TV showed a close-up of the face of a Korean man who was shooting a rifle. With his own people on the verge of being wiped out, he was the picture of ferocity. You could hear the sound of bullets ricocheting around him.

Yu found herself wondering how the Japanese would have behaved if this had happened in Little Tokyo. She didn't believe in gun ownership, but she couldn't help feeling awed by the toughness of these Koreans. The President of South Korea had immediately requested President Bush to ensure the safety of the 350,000 immigrants from his country.

She took a moment to think about whether the Japanese government would ever do such a thing. "The people living in Japan consider those of us who have gone out of the country to be *kimin*—people who have been cut off from the protection of the nation. We don't even have the right to vote. They probably wouldn't care if we were on the verge of being killed off."

One thing Yu had discovered after coming to America was that, compared to Chinese and Koreans, Japanese were really bad at socializing with people from other ethnic groups—perhaps because in Japan, they were all crowded together on their own islands. She herself had often become impatient with this trait. Thus, seeing Japan from the outside, she frequently felt frustrated at what the Japanese government said and did.

Though they were a long way from the rioting, they were still in the same city. Yu kept thinking that it might be best to bundle up everything they felt was important and put it in the car, but she was too petrified to make a move.

The announcer reported that a freelance reporter had been shot four times, the first time such a thing had ever happened to a journalist in Los Angeles.

Next there was an interview of a man with light black skin; he had swollen eyes and blood running from his forehead. "I always thought of myself as black, but just now, I was dragged out of my car by some black rioters and beaten with a club. I'm really shocked. I'm shocked at where they're drawing the color line. My family lives on Crenshaw in an area where there are lots of blacks. One of my grandmothers is white, but still . . ." he said, a look of bewilderment on his face as he wiped the blood from his forehead and gazed at the broken windows of his car.

When she saw this, Yu recalled something that her friend Michelle, who also had light black skin, had said. "It's not just whites who discriminate against people because of the color of their skin. Blacks do it, too, grading people according to how dark their skin is. My kids have fairly light skin, right? So some of the black mothers in our neighborhood asked me, 'Why is Monique white?' As if I'd committed some sort of crime. Well, you know, one of my ancestors was probably raped by a white plantation owner, so white blood got mixed in our blood line and sometimes shows up in the form of lighter skin color. It makes me mad how far people go in discriminating on the basis of the exact color of your skin." She had let out a big sigh and seemed pretty upset about it, but at the time, Yu had thought that she was just suffering delusions of grandeur. Now she realized that was not the case.

Yu wondered what the other Japanese mother whom she occasionally saw at Miki's elementary school was thinking now. This woman had stopped talking to Yu after Yu had explained to her how her own children were experiencing discrimination.

"You take things that way because you have an inferiority complex," the woman had said. Like Yu, she, too, was married to a Caucasian.

Yu had shot back, "I don't have any such thing. When you've lived here as long as I have, I think you at least know when someone is discriminating against you. If you don't feel it, you're just too obtuse to notice. I really get angry at people who discriminate against others."

169

"If you get angry so easily, people will think you weren't brought up properly. Please watch yourself."

Yu couldn't believe she had said that, so she told the woman off: "Oh? I should think that someone who didn't get angry at something like that would be the one who had a bad upbringing. Parents who don't teach their children to pay attention to what is right surely can't be said to have brought their children up properly, can they?"

After that, the other mother had not even said hello to Yu when they'd run into each other at school. She was always spouting ultra-conservative Republican rhetoric about how the large number of immigrants from Mexico, Vietnam and other places like that was having a bad impact on American society, and how blacks don't have much ability so it's a waste to pay a lot for their education. Yu figured that these were probably the woman's husband's ideas, and that this Japanese mother probably thought of herself as white.

But even if this woman was seen to be aligned with whites when she was with her husband, when she was walking down the street on her own, no one would know that she was married to a white man unless she wore a tag with her husband's name—or rather his race—written on it. She might even be taken for one of the Vietnamese she so despised. She really had too little imagination, thought Yu. But what would she be thinking about the riots? There would never be another day like today for raising a person's consciousness about the color of her skin.

"O-Yu-sama," said the voice on the phone. Yu's friend Nobuko always jokingly referred to Yu in this old-fashioned Japanese manner of address for women. Nobuko was the wife of a Japanese trading company employee, a plump woman who also lived in Santa Monica and seemed resigned to being there permanently. Like Yu, she was from the Kansai area, so Yu felt close to her.

"*Doushite-haru ka naa, to omotte*—I was wondering how you were doing," she began in her broad Kansai accent. "It's scary, isn't it? I haven't taken a step out of the house."

"Nobuko-san! How's your family? Is everyone okay?" inquired Yu.

"Yes, so far we're all right. But I'm worried. When will it quiet down? My husband's office is downtown, you know."

"Oh my goodness! Did he go to work?"

"Well, of course he did. Japanese trading companies don't close down at times like this. I don't suppose they'll get much work done, though. And it's dangerous. I think anyone who would go to work on a day like today is crazy! I even told him that, but do you think he'd listen? But more than that, I'm worried about something else: we just got our green cards a while back, but if things like this are going to happen, I think we need to reconsider."

"You guys are both Japanese, so I suppose you could go back and live out your lives in Japan, I don't think that's really a possibility for me anymore. Bob and the girls are Americans, after all."

"Well, it's been twelve years since we left Japan, you know. If we went back there now, we'd probably just feel caged in. Prices are high and the people are so picky, I'm not sure we could adapt to that way of life again. But say, did you hear? Rioters threw rocks at the windows in the lobby of the Hotel New Otani in Little Tokyo yesterday, and they broke a couple of the panes. It's really frightening! You know, the opening of the Japanese American National Museum was the same day, and I hear that former Prime Minister Kaifu, who came from Japan for the ceremony, was staying there. Apparently, none of the bigwig city officials like Mayor Bradley who were supposed to attend the ceremony showed up."

"Oh? Even though it's the one and only Japanese American museum in the country? Oh well—of all the times to have an opening!"

"You know what else happened? I heard this from a woman who works at another company, but anyway, her husband was driving on the Harbor Freeway—I guess he drives a Jeep—and a black guy goes out of his way to open his car window and starts yelling at him. I guess her husband was afraid the guy was going to do something to him. He was driving on the side of the freeway where there were buildings burning, so he had to drive through smoke, and it was hot and really awful. And according to her, people—not just from her company, but from other companies, too—want to make sure they're not mistaken for Koreans, so they're talking about pasting a Japanese flag on their car and writing 'Japanese' on it."

Yu was stunned by such an ignoble idea. But then she remembered that she had seen that kind of thing before. Where was it? Oh yes, she remembered now. Some Japanese children they had seen in Bombay, India—probably the children of Japanese who worked there—didn't they have Rising Sun flags on their chests? When she'd seen it, she hadn't understood what it meant—after all, they weren't in the Olympics or anything. But it was right after that that she'd been pelted with rocks in front of the Elephanta Caves. That's when she'd finally understood the meaning of the Japanese flags. But doing that certainly wouldn't make the real targets of their wrath feel good; it would probably make them feel like they were being totally abandoned.

She recalled that on that trip, she and Bob had gone into a Chinese restaurant where they were the only customers in the place. Surprised, they had asked why and been told by the embarrassed Chinese owner that due to the border war, people had stopped coming in because they were afraid. Yu recalled how sick and tired she'd been of spicy Indian food, and how delicious she'd thought that Chinese food was.

There's a story told about how the King of Denmark, upon learning that the Nazis were making Jews wear a yellow Star of David on their chest to mark them so that they could be persecuted more easily, put a yellow star on his own chest, but the Japanese here were working from exactly the opposite mind-set.

"At times like this, flags won't do any good," Yu argued. "The rioters probably have no idea what the flags of the Philippines, China and Korea look like, or the Japanese flag, for that matter. I'm not sure I could distinguish them, either. All they know is the color of your face. And if they did recognize the Japanese flag, it would probably only be because we were enemies during the war, so they'd think we were bad guys, wouldn't they?"

As soon as she had blurted that out, Yu became much less sure of herself. Who was she to judge? If you could save your life by displaying a Japanese flag, maybe that was all right for people who didn't feel at all guilty about doing so. In the end, war was like that, too, if you considered the end result: It was the people who managed to survive somehow that won out. If you died, that was the end.

During the War, when Japanese Americans were being taken away to internment camps and their assets were being seized, they say that the Chinese in San Francisco all hung Chinese flags in front of their stores. To those who were sent to the internment camps, the sight of those flags must have been painful. Realizing that the people who'd been your friends the day before could come up with an idea like that would make you feel completely abandoned. Still, how could you blame them? Their lives were on the line.

The television showed people looting in broad daylight. They were taking beds and other large pieces of furniture. Which must mean that they were carrying them away to trucks they had brought with this in mind. At this point, Latinos were by far the largest group of looters. A few whites and Asians could even be seen. These people were nothing more than opportunists.

The looters would steal everything in a shop and then when it was empty, set it on fire. Gradually, however, the crowds had begun to concentrate on stealing, perhaps because they felt it was too much trouble to set fires, or perhaps because they had a different goal than those who had started the riots. It looked like they didn't want to put their own safety at risk by starting fires; they must have felt that since everyone else was looting, it would be their own loss if they didn't steal something, too.

A couple of short Latino men hoisted a large sofa piled high with children's clothes, women's dresses and men's suits out through a broken show window and onto the sidewalk, where gangs of looters roamed through scattered trash and broken glass. Just at that moment, a police car arrived on the scene. The crowd dispersed in all directions like so many baby spiders. The sofa piled with clothing was left right where it had been flung onto the sidewalk.

The camera panned over to the grand entrance of the store. "I've seen that building before," Yu thought. She began searching the screen for clues as to which establishment it was. It was the Bullock's Wilshire department store! She'd been there just three days earlier! She'd never dreamed that that elegant storefront would be so horribly transfigured in just three days' time.

The image converged with sights she had seen during the war. Buildings that had been standing the day before would disappear without a trace in the air raids, or would be transformed into ashes, with only the steel skeleton and burnt wooden piles left standing in the wreckage. And the night skies dappled with flying sparks . . .

She realized that no matter where they lived, people had no guarantee that it would always be peaceful. People who were in Japan now—like Miki—were maybe better off. At least for now.

The phone rang. It was Meg's husband Tom, a producer of commercials. "Yu, are you all okay?"

"Yeah. We're all right. Thanks."

"Did you see the looting on TV?"

"I'm watching it right now. They were taking out heaps of furniture."

"As long as they're taking stuff, you'd think they'd show better taste. Everything the jerks are making off with is so tacky."

The way he was talking, you'd have thought he was watching a football game—something he often did while talking to Bob on the phone.

Realizing that Tom probably didn't have a clue as to the actual situation the have-nots were facing, Yu tried to enlighten him. "I suppose that they don't have anything, and must not have time to be choosy. They might not have chairs to sit in or beds to sleep in."

The camera took in the expanse of Wilshire Boulevard at night. A dusk-to-dawn curfew was in place, so cars were out only in the most desperate of circumstances. Everyone was being checked. Of course, even without the curfew, ordinary people wouldn't even think of going out at a time like this. The wide street normally overflowed with cars, but none could be seen on it now. In their place, fire engines and police cars regularly raced down the unlit thoroughfare, their sirens wailing.

7

Yu was caught up watching the riots on TV when she heard the sound of the door opening behind her.

"My right shoulder hurts," said Bob in a drooping voice.

When Yu turned around to look at him, she could see that his white hair was disheveled and his left hand was on his right shoulder.

Why at a time like this? Yu was brought back to the reality of her own home as she took a good look at Bob's anxious face. Whenever anyone mentioned pain in their shoulders or arms, she immediately thought it was connected to their heart, since a doctor had once told her that if someone with heart problems said that the back of their neck hurt or their shoulders or arms suddenly felt constricted, you should assume that they're having a heart attack.

She therefore did not check to determine whether Bob felt the pain when he moved his arm or if it was there even when he wasn't doing anything; she assumed that he was having a heart attack and that she should get him to the hospital immediately. However, judging from the news she'd just been watching, she was also sure that the hospitals were overrun with people who'd been injured in the riots. The two thoughts collided in her brain. The end result was that she became preoccupied by one simple thought: "I don't know what to do!" This plunged her into a state of complete paralysis.

"There won't be any doctors there anyway," she thought. "They're probably all out taking care of people on the street." Finally, despite her confusion, Yu blurted out, "It's your heart, isn't it? We've got to call a doctor . . ."

"No. It's *not* my heart." Holding his hand up to his shoulder, Bob backed away as he spoke.

"What's the phone number? Dr. Robinson's phone number?" Yu crouched down as she spoke.

"No, I'll call," said Bob as he slowly made his way to the bedroom, dragging his leg.

It was almost midnight, but the television kept repeating the news about the fires and looting.

Just as she'd thought, their family doctor wasn't in. After a while, the doctor on call contacted them. It was not someone they knew. He listened to Bob's symptoms and then said, "I don't think it's your heart, but I can't tell for sure over the phone, so you should go to a hospital emergency room. The hospitals are having a tough time today, but still . . ."

When he heard that, Bob felt like all the blood was draining out of his head. Imagine telling someone to go to a hospital emergency room on a night like this . . . When he told this to Yu, she said in a worried voice, "We'd better go. I'll drive."

"I'm not going," said Bob, shaking his head. "I refuse."

Going out with Yu—who was not a very good driver—at the wheel, at this late hour, and when there was a curfew on to boot? When there were rioters wandering around with guns? There was no way to tell which choice was more dangerous to life and limb.

"Ah . . . I feel a little queasy," murmured Bob as he began rubbing his chest.

To make sure she was remembering things correctly, Yu went to the living room and pulled a medical reference book off the bookshelf. Donning her reading glasses, she hastily turned the pages. Her eyes wildly darted around the text. At last she found the heart column.

> Sudden, severe pain in the anterior thorax. Tightness of the chest or splitting pain . . . Also, cold sweat, nausea, heartburn, diarrhea, etc. Loss of consciousness in some elderly patients.

"Oops, that was myocardial infarction." Yu went on to read the next entry: angina pectoris.

> Often experienced as chest discomfort, or a feeling of tightness or pressure rather than pain, centering on the anterior thorax, but frequently with pain and numbness radiating from the left shoulder to the inner left arm and sometimes to the neck, jaw, upper abdomen and back. Take nitroglycerin as a precaution.

Yu thought Bob had mentioned his right shoulder. And hadn't he mentioned feeling nauseous just now? That would make it myocardial infarction—a heart attack?

"Hey, is it your right shoulder—or your left?" she yelled as she came back down the hallway. There was no answer. He wasn't in the bedroom. She noticed that there was a light on in the bathroom, which had wallpaper with a green arabesque pattern dotted with red flowers. She quickly went inside.

Bob was sitting on the toilet, his eyes half closed. His complexion was ashen, his penis dangling limply.

"I've got the runs," he murmured in a voice so weak it sounded like a mosquito buzzing. His body was rigid, and he didn't move. He looked like he might be dying. Even so, his heart didn't hurt . . .

The runs? Diarrhea was a sign of myocardial infarction. Yu tried to wipe his bottom for him by reaching over to take some toilet paper with her right hand while trying to support him with her left, but before she could do so, he toppled onto the floor and lay there unconscious. His hand felt cold to the touch. Worried that he might have died, Yu called in a loud voice, "Bob! Bob!"

He didn't respond.

She felt like she'd been doused with cold water, and suddenly, the bathroom wallpaper looked white, as if the green and red had suddenly been bleached out. Her whole body drooped, seemingly drained of all strength. She held her breath and stared at Bob for some time, but then, realizing that she couldn't leave things as they were, she collected herself and, pulling on Bob's arms, tried to raise him up. He didn't move. She realized that there was no way she could carry him alone. Yet even if she called an ambulance, it probably would take forever to come on a night like tonight . . .

"Is he dead?" No sooner had she thought that than Yu's heart pounding wildly. Trying to quiet it, she began to take slow, deep breaths.

"Nothing is going to be solved if I collapse now," she thought. "Or will it? Maybe it would be better if we both went down together.

"Is this it—is he really dying? The moment I've always feared? If it is—what a time! What a place! My sister-in-law died in a bathroom. Now her younger brother is dying in one, too—they sure picked a gross place! Well, I guess it's not like they really had a choice."

Lost in a fog, Yu stared straight ahead at the glass doors of the shower, which were covered in soap scum. "What am I supposed to do now?" she wondered. She could feel her brow furrow. "Maybe I should call the girls in Tokyo and Rome. Miki almost never says, 'I love you,' and when she does, this is what happens."

After a time, Yu remembered something she'd heard from a friend of hers in the neighborhood who had recently been widowed: "This is really important: If your husband dies, you mustn't panic—even if you're really sad. At a time like this, you should not get sentimental. Even before you let the doctor know, the very first thing you need to do is go to the bank and take out a large sum of money. If you don't, the money will be frozen in your account until the estate taxes are paid. From the following day, you won't have any money to live on. I didn't know that, and I had a terrible time."

Yu pondered that advice, then swallowed and took another deep breath to try to calm herself. Then she looked down again at her husband, who was lying on the floor. His glasses were askew and there were beads of sweat on his forehead. He was pallid, unmoving.

Yu did her best to control herself. She vowed not to cry. Should she leave the body here like this and go to the bank? No, she couldn't go get money out of the bank now, in the midst of riots like this.

There was no cash in the house . . . She always made sure she had fifty dollars in her purse because in this country, there was always the possibility that you could be held up when you went out, and if you didn't have any cash on you, you might be killed, but she had no idea how much Bob might have in his wallet.

Yu started to feel dizzy. She figured that what her friend had told her was true. With just fifty dollars, she couldn't possibly live for a month. But she had no idea how much she should withdraw. She'd always left the banking to Bob, so she didn't even know which bank to go to. If only Miki or Ann were here now!

Yu had been standing in the middle of the bathroom this whole time. She should go look for the checks. She had her own personal checks in her purse, but it was the joint account that had most of the money in it.

She rushed out of the bathroom and over to the table in the hallway and quickly opened the drawer in which they kept their checkbooks and bank statements. In one corner there was a photograph. It was of the two of them and had been taken during their first year of marriage while they were traveling in Italy. They were standing in front of the Baths of Caracalla in Rome, wearing jeans and smiling. They both looked young and radiant and full of life. Yu thought it strange that this photo should be in here . . .

She suddenly recalled how much fun she'd had the day she'd first met Bob. It was in 1961, during her second year in the United States, when she'd finally become accustomed to living in New York. While on a walk, she happened to make her way to Central Park and had sat herself down on a bench in the warm sunlight, reading *The Second Sex* by Simone de Beauvoir. Just the day before, her roommate Carol, who worked for a news magazine, had told her all about the book.

"When *The Second Sex* first came out, the reviews in America were not good. The reviewers in America are all men and one of them, a well-known male reviewer wrote, 'The book may be true in France, but it seems old-fashioned in America, since American women are all free and liberated.' Even though he was a womanizer, he was famous, so other men envied him. That's why his evaluation became accepted as standard. Ten years have passed since then, and even now, someone like me who studied at college alongside men may spend the rest of her life as a secretary—that's something to think about."

Her words had surprised Yu, who until that time had believed that American women worked alongside men as equals. Yu had read the Japanese translation of Beauvoir's work many years earlier, but she decided to take a closer look at the status of women in America, so she borrowed the English translation from the library and had just started to read it. At the time, she had known almost nothing about American society. Later on, when people said that women had gained in stature, they were mainly talking about white women, completely ignoring the status of minority women,

That had been thirty-one years earlier, on May 5. The temperature had been perfect—and the trees were covered in fresh new leaves. A cheerful mood wafted in the air, sweeping away the gloom of the long New York winter.

With tussled chestnut brown hair and a face like a melancholic Jack Lemmon, Bob came and sat down on the bench where Yu was reading. His heart had just been broken; he was brooding and didn't even notice Yu sitting next to him. However, some pollen must have gotten into her nose: She sneezed five times in quick succession.

"God bless you," he said.

"I don't believe in God." Yu's frank but unusual response had been the catalyst that had sparked their romance.

At the time, Bob didn't realize that she was Japanese. Afterward, he excused his use of the clichéd phrase by saying that he realized she was Asian and figured that using a set expression would make it easier for her to understand. He'd never dreamed that an Asian could be so cantankerous as to sound off like that when a simple 'thank you' would have sufficed, and that obstinacy of hers piqued his curiosity. His acceptance of her, in turn, made Yu feel that they might be similar in temperament.

Oh, those tender, warm embraces! Ecstasy strong enough to melt you! Truly creative lovemaking! There was a moment when she'd been so intoxicated with it all that she thought this must be what they mean by ambrosia and nectar—the food and drink of the gods.

At that time, she never dreamed that she'd ever face the kind of situation she was in now. She'd believed that ecstasy would last forever.

Now, it was all over. If only she hadn't said those awful things to him the other day!

"Could you wipe my ass for me?" a coarse whisper came from the bathroom floor.

Yu rushed into the bathroom as Bob was wriggling himself up. He wasn't dead after all!

Yu thought back to the lists of symptoms she'd read earlier. What Bob described was a combination of the symptoms of cardiac infarction and angina pectoris. The pain was on the right side rather than the left, but she figured it would be best to be safe.

"Don't you think we should go to the hospital?" Yu wiped his bottom, made him put on underwear, got him dressed and kept urging him to seek help. Bob, meanwhile, was abnormally quiet. Eerily so.

Weakly he said, "I'm not going."

"Yes, you are. It's best to be sure," Yu asserted firmly.

All the same, she felt unsure, though it was for an entirely different reason. There was a dusk-to-dawn curfew on, so there was no telling when or where they might be stopped by the police. And since she was Asian, she might be mistaken for a Korean and attacked by some blacks. The roads would be empty, though, so at least they could drive quickly.

Bob's color had improved, so they slowly made their way to the garage. Bob said he would drive, but Yu, worried that he might lose consciousness again, insisted on doing it herself.

8

Sunset Boulevard was silent—not a car on it. Yet just a few miles east on this very road, there were stores with their windows broken, insides trashed, and set afire. The air was chilly, but Yu's cheeks were hot.

They turned down the steep slope of Chautauqua Boulevard. About halfway down the hill, Yu could see that the traffic light at the bottom had turned yellow. The light was at a junction where Chautaqua fed into the Coast Highway, making a forty-degree turn there. Yu figured that if she picked up any more speed going downhill, she'd never be able to negotiate the sharp turn. Fearing that the car might flip over, she decided to stop and stepped on the brake hard, screeching to a halt.

Suddenly Bob, who had been quiet in the passenger seat, shrilly shouted, "Why are you stopping? We have to wait five minutes for the light to change. My heart won't hold out that long!"

"Yelling like that is bad for your heart. Instead of crashing and getting us both killed, it'd be better if only one of us dies!"

Shocked at the cruelty of her own words, Yu nonetheless tried to justify them. "The two of us can't die together. Neither one of the girls is able to live on her own yet." She was shouting

185

almost as loud as Bob had. It felt like it might be *her* heart that would give out.

Though she had used the girls as her excuse, her real reason for not wanting to be involved in behavior that was tantamount to double suicide at this point in her life was that she was at last starting to do work that she liked and was getting back on track with her career.

She opened the driver's side window. The wind off the ocean came rushing in and cooled her hot, throbbing head. The fragrance of night-blooming jasmine drifted in from somewhere.

"I'm not a kamikaze pilot!" Yu yelled, tightly squeezing the steering wheel and looking straight ahead, as if the words were not directed at anyone in particular. Her voice echoed in the darkness, reverberating off the cliff that soared above them on the hill side of the road. In front of her, the expanse of the Pacific Coast Highway lay in silence, its six lanes—which were normally filled with a steady stream of cars—completely empty. Beyond that lay the vast Pacific Ocean. She could faintly hear its roar now, even though she had never heard it here before.

"If he could yell that loud, his heart must be all right," thought Yu.

Suddenly a police car slipped into the right lane and stopped. A black policeman was inside. Thinking that they would be interrogated, Yu became even more anxious, but the officer was busy answering his radio and didn't even get out of the car. Since from this lane she couldn't have turned back even if she'd wanted to, Yu decided to go on to the hospital.

They finally reached the hospital on Santa Monica Boulevard, but Yu was intimidated by the steady stream of police cars, ambulances and private cars turning into the crescent-shaped driveway. She parked carefully, making sure not to hit another car. Standing in that dark spot and looking over at the brilliantly lit emergency entrance of the hospital, she felt like a spectator watching a staged battle-scene. No sooner had they arrived than a patient was taken out of an ambulance and laid directly on the pavement, where he was given mouth-to-mouth resuscitation, while another—a black man who appeared to be on the verge of death due to massive blood loss, possibly from a gunshot wound—was carried out of the ambulance on a stretcher, an IV tube in his arm, accompanied by a nurse holding pouches of medicine. There was also a young white woman who appeared to have cut her hand on broken glass, as well as a youth who had a bloody bandage wrapped around his leg and couldn't walk without the support of two male nurses wearing pale green jackets. An elderly patient had been left slumped in a wheelchair at the hospital entrance. Appalling. It was just like a blood-drenched battlefield hospital.

Looking upon the scene, Yu began to tremble. She hadn't the faintest idea how to deal with this. There was no way they could have Bob examined here. What could they do? Bob, who had also caught a glimpse of what was going on at the hospital entrance, said in a small, trembling voice, "Let's go home. I'm all right."

"Your chest doesn't hurt?"

"No."

"How about the back of your neck?"

"That never hurt. And it was my right shoulder that hurt—not my left."

"Oh? So why did you break out in a cold sweat and black out back there? I don't get it. I thought you were going to die."

"When I was talking to the doctor, there was all that talk about my heart and the emergency room, and when I thought about going to the hospital while a riot was going on, I panicked. I guess I had a panic attack, felt faint, and ended up like that."

On the way home, Bob said he'd drive and then raced all the way at such a crazy speed that Yu become so frightened she could scarcely breathe.

At last she felt some relief, but all the same, Yu worried about Bob's breathing even while they were sleeping and kept putting her hand under his nose to check to make sure that it had not stopped. Finally, Bob bellowed, "You're driving me crazy! I'm sleepy. Let me rest!"

9

May 1

The next morning, Bob was still alive. But he was complaining that when he moved his right shoulder, it hurt so much it made him jump.

Yu looked at the day's *Los Angeles Times* on the dining room table.

The first thing she noticed was a large photo of dozens of looters who had been arrested and were lying on the ground with their hands tied behind their backs like so many tuna lined up for auction at Tokyo's Tsukiji wholesale fish market. "That's just the tip of the iceberg," Yu thought. "There's no way they could arrest all the people who took part in the rioting and looting—there were just too many."

The *Los Angeles Times* headline read:

```
Looting and Fires Ravage L.A. / 25 Dead,
572 Injured, 1,000 Blazes
```

On television, there was a report that President Bush had ordered four or five hundred Marines and Army infantrymen be sent to the area.

It all seemed too late. Both the police and the federal government had been tardy in taking action. If their measures had come a day earlier, there wouldn't have been this much damage, Yu thought.

There was also a report that many sporting goods stores had been looted and that the looters had made off with all of the shotguns they had in stock. If the guns fell into the hands of the 90,000 or so gang members in the city, it might set the stage for guerilla warfare. Once looted, guns were not likely to be returned. Even if the rioting were suppressed, the city was obviously going to become more dangerous. How could they possibly find all the weapons that had been stolen during all this confusion?

The fires were moving further west.

Meg phoned.

"Yu-hoo-hoo! Listen. There was rioting in Venice yesterday. It's gotten that far already. Did you know that?"

"No, I didn't. Venice—isn't that just south of Santa Monica? Oh no!"

"And you know what else? I hear Dr. Robinson's son joined in the looting and brought back a television. And then I guess he got caught by the police." She sounded so pleased with herself you might have thought she had caught the devil himself.

"Really? Such a rich man's kid?" Yu was so stunned she couldn't speak for a moment. Finally she said, "No wonder Dr. Robinson wasn't at home yesterday."

"What? You called him yesterday?"

"Yeah. Bob's heart . . . turns out it was nothing."

"Oh? You should call us at times like that. We're always willing to help. That's what friends are for."

"Thanks." With no relatives or children living in the same city, Yu had been feeling insecure, but Meg's kind words reassured her.

10

While they were on the phone, Bob had asked to speak to Meg's husband Tom, and when he happened to mention the pain he'd been feeling from his shoulder into his arm, Tom told him that a friend of his was a chiropractor who treated athletes and offered to take Bob to see him, so off they went.

It turned out that Bob had strained a muscle. Yu was relieved to learn that the problem wasn't his heart. Maybe that was why she had also forgotten her fear of people not being able to tell the difference between Koreans and Japanese.

It seems that the problem with Bob's shoulder had developed when Yu had sent him to the supermarket and he'd come back carrying those four heavy bags of food all at once. Of course, it was his fault for not having called Yu and asked her to help. He also could have prevented this by dividing up the groceries into smaller lots. In any case, the real problem was that he wasn't taking his own age into consideration. So no matter how you looked at it, Bob was to blame. Even so, Yu *had* been the one who'd asked him to go, and for that, she felt a little guilty, so she was doing a lot of running around for him.

The first thing they needed was a hot water bottle. They

didn't have one in the house, so she ran out to the drugstore to get one. It was actually a bag made out of rubber into which hot water could be poured for use in heating a specific area of the body. In Japan, this kind of thing is called a cool water pillow and people put ice in it. Yu was struck by the contrast: a perfect example of the Japanese adage of "things change with the place."

After that, Yu made her way to the packed supermarket to pick up food items that Bob had forgotten to get the previous day. And then there was the mountain of laundry that had piled up during the two full days that she had been glued to the television set.

Her thoughts then turned to the design she was supposed to finish, and she recalled that the factory that had placed the order for it was in East Los Angeles. She began to worry about whether or not it had been damaged in the riots.

The chiropractor had recommended that Bob put ice in a plastic bag and keep it on his shoulder for a while. Then he should do the same thing with a bag filled with hot water and keep alternating the two bags over a period of two hours. Then after an hour's break, he should repeat the process of alternating the cold and hot water packs for another two hours.

Yu took out all of the ice in the freezer and put it in a plastic bag, then dug an old rubber band out of a drawer and wrapped it repeatedly around the mouth of the bag to make sure that no water would leak out. After pouring some water into a kettle and putting it on the stove to heat it up, she took the bag full of ice into the bedroom.

She tried to put it on Bob's shoulder, but no matter whether he was standing or sitting, he couldn't stay still with it on his shoulder for ten minutes. Out of desperation, he tried lying on the bed, his head down at the foot of the bed and his arm dangling over the edge. When Yu placed the big ice pack on his shoulder, Bob screamed, "Ow! Gently! So it won't slide off. I'm in pain and can't get up easily. So make sure it won't fall. Have you got the next pack ready? It's got to be hot. Boil it, okay?"

"What? Boiling? Really?" Yu was uncertain as she returned to the kitchen.

The kettle wasn't boiling yet. "But hold on," she thought. "If I boil this, how can I get it into the rubber bag? I'll end up burning myself, or the water will melt the rubber, or Bob's shoulder will get burned." The teakettle started to whistle, so she turned the burner off.

At last she had a little time for herself, so she made her way to the toilet in their bedroom. No sooner had she gotten inside than Bob yelled, "What happened to the hot water? The time for the ice pack is over. He said exactly ten minutes."

Startled, Yu rushed out of the bathroom. Bob was lying face down, so his voice sounded like he was being strangled and the blue lines of his veins could be clearly seen on his temple.

"Can't I go to the bathroom in peace? The water started boiling quite a while ago, so I turned off the burner." She took a breath, then continued. "Ten minutes, twelve minutes—what's the difference? This is ridiculous!"

"No, you've got to do this kind of thing properly. It's like a recipe. You know the reason why you can't bake bread or make a cake is because you don't follow the recipe." Since Bob was lying on his stomach, his words were hard to make out. But Yu was only half listening anyway. She was on her way out of the room when she heard a grumbling noise like he was trying to say something more.

"I can't read anything in this position and I'm bored. Could you turn on the TV for me? I've been saying that for a while now . . ."

Yu went back and hurriedly turned on the TV. It seemed

rather loud, but she left it that way.

Back in the kitchen, she opened the mouth of the brown hot water bottle and poured in hot water from the kettle. The temperature was a little above lukewarm. "This will do," thought Yu. "It's just . . . comfortable."

Next, she opened the freezer to see if there was any ice for the next stage, but it was all gone. "Uh oh. I wasn't thinking when I used it all up. Well, there's no way I can make more in ten minutes. If he knew this, he'd get mad. What to do?"

She began rummaging around in the freezer and found a chunk of frozen peeled ginger root covered with frost and stored in a freezer bag, and then, among the chicken, *mochi* rice cakes, fish, bread and other frozen foods, she discovered a small blue bag.

"Oh—perfect!" she thought. It was a pack of Blue Ice that they had used years ago when the children were little. It stays cold for a very long time. "What a relief! Well, that's one thing out of the way."

She took the bag full of hot water to Bob, removed the bag of half-melted ice from his shoulder and was about to put the bag of hot water in its place when Bob asked, "Did you boil the water?"

"Do you think you could put boiling water in this rubber bag? It would melt, and you would get a burn—and I'd get burned when I poured it in!" Yu was not the kind of person who could keep up a falsehood, so she always told him the truth—and that meant that things always got complicated.

"The box the hot water bottle came in must have had a warning label. Bring it here." He never trusted her with machinery or technical things. He must have thought she was crazy to believe that water that wasn't boiling could be an effective treatment.

Yu went to the kitchen and quickly brought back the warning label. As she handed it to Bob, she wondered, 'Does he really not realize that he's asking me to do something that flies in the face of basic scientific principles?'

"Hmm. It does say, 'Don't use boiling water.'"

"Of course it does! Anyone with common sense would know that, even without reading the label! You have almost no knowledge of science, and yet you never believe what I say. You always have to ask someone else. It's ridiculous!"

"In that case, you could just use the hot water from the sink, couldn't you."

Yu realized he was right. Perhaps he wasn't a complete idiot.

Ten minutes had passed. Yu brought in the Blue Ice and exchanged it for the hot water bottle.

"What's that blue thing?" Bob looked at the ice pack as if he felt it were rather disgusting.

"It's Blue Ice. Remember, we used to take it along on picnics when the girls were little? It's a kind of ice."

"I don't want that. I want regular ice."

"It's all gone, so we have to use this."

"Why don't you always have ice on hand?"

"We don't drink alcohol all that much, so I don't make a lot. And I put all we had in that first bag, so we're all out. You can't make more in ten minutes. Even if this is blue, it lasts a long time and it's just like ice. There's no law against making use of modern conveniences, is there?"

The television at the foot of the bed was still turned on loud, since Bob couldn't get up to adjust the sound. The two of them were shouting so as to be heard over the noise. The images on the screen were the same as before: burning buildings.

Yu was thinking about her design again. It was almost done when the riots began, and now, she wasn't even sure if the client still existed, so maybe there was no need to hurry . . . All the same, she didn't like to break a promise. Yet the way things were going, there was no telling when Bob would set her free—when she'd be able to get back to work . . .

She started to feel faint. "What time was it when I finally got to bed last night? Three in the morning? I'm not young anymore. Got to watch out . . . I was so worried about Bob that I couldn't sleep."

Yu noticed that she was hungry. It was already one o'clock. Trying to figure out what to eat, she opened the refrigerator door and began rummaging around for something that would do for lunch.

"Hey . . . it." She could hear Bob yelling in the bedroom but could not make out what he was saying.

She hastily closed the refrigerator and rushed into the bedroom to see what Bob wanted. He told her he thought it might be better to have a T-shirt on instead of having the hot and cold water bags directly on his bare skin. Since his shoulder was in pain, he couldn't move his arms and needed help to put one on. However, when Yu tried to lift his arms up just a little, he screamed that it hurt.

It was no easy task to get a T-shirt on such a big body. When he at last had it on, Yu straightened up. Suddenly, she felt a sharp pain in her back—an area that hadn't bothered her for a year now. Beads of sweat formed on her forehead and she could feel her pulse racing through her temple. She was exhausted.

11

"I have to get something to eat or my body won't hold out. Running around like this . . . Bob has been lying down this whole time, so I suppose he isn't hungry. I'll eat first. Oh —there's some udon."

As she made the Japanese noodle soup, Yu kept rubbing her back with her right hand. First she made the soup stock, then she simmered the sliced kamaboko fish paste and shiitake mushrooms in a sweetened soy broth and chopped the spring onions. Just when she had finally seated herself at the dining room table and was blowing on the soup to cool it off, Bob appeared. Seeing that Yu was eating, he blurted out, "Hey— what's this? You leave me alone and eat? How come you didn't make me some and then call me?"

Now that she thought about it, it was time for the break after two hours of treatment.

"What with the shopping this morning and then running around bringing you hot water and ice every ten minutes, I'm all worn out and hungry . . . So I'm eating first. And on top of that, my back pain has come back! Do you need any more excuses?"

"Boy, you're unfeeling! I mean, how cruel can you

be—making lunch for yourself and not letting anyone else eat!"
As he was yelling, Bob pulled out a chair, but instead of using
his left hand, he used his right. "Yeow," he bellowed, and tum-
bled onto the floor.

That seemed a little extreme to Yu. Why did he fall down if
his arm hurt? Nonetheless, she put down her chopsticks and,
sticking her hands under his arms, hoisted him up onto the
chair next to hers. Then, rubbing her back with her right hand,
she sat back down.

"You know, you've been lying around all morning, so I figured you wouldn't be hungry. And you might even have been
asleep. First, the caretaker needs to eat. And so what if ten minutes becomes twelve? Running around yelling like that! Hasn't
past experience taught you that doing exactly what doctors and
scholars say doesn't make any difference? All of it is just based on
hypotheses, isn't it?" As she spoke, Yu's feelings became stronger
and anger welled up inside her; her eyes opened wide, and she
pounded on the table with her fist.

Then, in a high-pitched voice, she declared: "You know, I'm
from a minority, too—just like those people!" She was yelling
so loudly she thought she might rupture the membranes in her
throat. "Where else in the world would they take a nurse who's
pushing sixty and boss her around like this, making her run
around doing all sorts of dirty work! You want to know what the
cause of these riots is? It's the arrogance of WASP males like you
who don't show any consideration for minorities whatsoever!"

As she was screaming this in a loud voice, Yu realized that
she had used one of those taboo stereotype terms about her
spouse, and she felt ashamed. However, her anger got the better
of her and, feeling that she couldn't very well back down at this
point, she went into the kitchen, opened a drawer and took out
a cigarette lighter that hadn't been used in years. Bob stared at

the lighter.

"So what if I eat a little bit earlier than you? Yesterday you passed out and had to be taken to the hospital; today, you needed ice and hot water packs changed ten times. I'm not thirty years old! If you go around shrieking and ordering me around like a slave, I'm going to start a riot right here. I'll burn this house down!" As she yelled this, Yu went out into the hallway and clawed at a pile of newspapers that had been stacked up for recycling and limped back to the dining room table with a newspaper in her hand.

Taking it in both hands, she wound it up into a tube and sat down. With the newspaper in her left hand and the lighter in her right, she clicked the lighter a number of times before it lit. Slowly, she brought the flame over to the top of the paper tube in her left hand. Soon the paper was blazing red. Black soot rose to the ceiling, and the dining room was filled with smoke.

The TV at the front of the room showed another group of small Latino men streaming up to a broken show window, taking out the cameras, camcorders, tripods, and binoculars that were on display inside and walking away with both arms full. The shop next door appeared to be a food store. It was already enveloped in flames. The announcer said that this was Vermont Avenue. That was in Hollywood.

Bob looked over at the TV. Then he looked back and forth a number of times, comparing the burning streets on the screen with the burning newspaper in Yu's hand. Swallowing, he became quiet.

The color of the flames on the television screen caught Yu's eye. "Huh? That's the street where Michelle lives. Fiona's office isn't all that far from there either."

Suddenly the phone—which was next to the TV—rang, breaking the tension between the two of them. The newspaper burning in her hand made it impossible for Yu to move, so she ignored the phone. After it had rung a number of times, Bob slowly moved over and picked it up.

"Hello. Oh, Ann, my love. How are you?" His face was flushed and he was talking in a loud voice. He may well have felt that Ann was his savior.

"How're you doing, Daddy? The riots have me so worried. Are you all right? How about Mommy?" Having no idea about what was actually going on, Ann peppered him with questions in the cheery voice she normally used.

Bob hesitated for a moment, then glanced at Yu and said, "Fine. Mommy's fine, too. No need to worry. The h-house is fine, too." As he added "the house," Bob stuttered and his face twitched.

The flame on the newspaper was making its way down toward Yu's hand, and she could now feel the heat. After hours of watching the virtual flames on television, now she was experiencing the reality of fire.

The television showed a shabbily dressed Latino man talking through an interpreter. "Once, I was two cents short of the price of a piece of meat and the butcher wouldn't sell it to me. It made me so angry. I'll never forget that. So I went into his shop with the looters and took a sheep. My friends and I barbecued it and ate it. It tasted wonderful. This is the least I can do to get revenge."

May 2, 1992

Los Angeles Times headlines:
```
Bush Ordering Troops to L.A.
```

```
Residents demand to know why it took so
long for troops to begin protecting them
Arriving Marines, Army troops voice con-
cerns about confronting fellow Americans
in South L.A. with bayonets like they
used in Panama and Iraq
Deaths placed at 40 ... injury total is 1,899
```

May 3, 1992

Los Angeles Times headlines:
```
Jittery L.A. Sees Rays of Hope
Few Crimes or Major Incidents Are Reported
Aftermath: With 45 deaths, riots become
the worst in contemporary U.S. History
```

The newspaper also reported that Korean children and black children who had previously played together had lost their trust in each other since the riots.

May 10, 1992

Los Angeles Times:
```
THE DEAD
In total, 58 people died as a result of
the rioting, according to the coroner as
of Saturday afternoon. The first fatal-
ity occurred at 8:15 p.m. Wednesday, and
the last known death occurred at 10:05
p.m. Sunday. Here is a breakdown: Race:
Black: 26 Latino: 18 White: 10 Asian: 2
Unknown: 2
```

```
Method: Gunshot: 41 Traffic/Accident: 7
Arson: 3 Natural: 1 Assault: 2 Other: 4
```

"We might have ended up in at least two different "Method" categories," murmured Yu as she read the paper.

"'Living' is the process of continuously protecting oneself from death, and it starts the instant one receives life in this world. *Honma ni shindoi koto ya wa*—It's really exhausting!"

The sound of Rodney King's voice as he drawled, "Can we all get along?" was still going around and around in Yu's head.

FOUMIKO KOMETANI was born in Osaka in 1930. A longtime resident of the US, she began her career as an abstract painter before turning to writing. She won the Akutagawa Prize in 1985.

MARY GOEBEL NOGUCHI is a Professor of English Linguistics in the Faculty of Letters at Kansai University, as well as the translator of Sadako Sawamura's *My Japanese Kitchen*.

SELECTED DALKEY ARCHIVE TITLES

FOR A FULL LIST OF PUBLICATIONS, VISIT:
www.dalkeyarchive.com

SELECTED DALKEY ARCHIVE TITLES

FOR A FULL LIST OF PUBLICATIONS, VISIT:
www.dalkeyarchive.com

SELECTED DALKEY ARCHIVE TITLES